DEATH IN THE MUSEUM OF MODERN ART

Death in the Museum of Modern Art
Six stories by Alma Lazarevska

Translated from the Bosnian by Celia Hawkesworth

First published in 2014 by
Istros Books
London, United Kingdom
www.istrosbooks.com

©Alma Lazarevska 2014
Translation ©Celia Hawkesworth, 2014
Artwork & Design@Milos Miljkovich, 2013
Graphic Designer/Web Developer -
miljkovicmisa@gmail.com

The right of Alma Lazarevska to be identified as the author
of this work has been asserted in accordance with the
Copyright, Designs and Patents Act, 1988

ISBN: 978-1908236173

Printed in England by
CMP (UK), Poole, Dorset

Supported using public funding by
ARTS COUNCIL
ENGLAND

Cover photo, 'Little Owl', an original print by Chris Cockburn
www.chriscockburn.co.uk

CONTENTS

DAFNA PEHFOGL CROSSES THE BRIDGE BETWEEN THERE AND HERE

At last the crossing was agreed. The young man who brought the good news did not bang roughly on the door. Nor did he shove her small, thin person arrogantly aside, as all the others before him had done, barging into the flat without taking off their boots. He had timid eyes, which she recognised, and he bowed before she confirmed that she had understood when and how the crossing would take place. She opened her mouth to offer him a glass of water and a sugared rose, but he was no longer outside the door.

'What a sweet cop,' she murmured.

Everything had to be done quietly, with as few witnesses as possible. Crossings of this kind were prohibited.

Months had passed in anticipation since the day when telephone links were severed between this side and that. The bridge between the two banks of the river was now crossed only by an occasional stray cat or street dog. But she had known that her family on the other side would do all in their power to bring her over, bless them. And even now, the night before her crossing, when she thought of them and touched the ring finger on her left hand, she felt ashamed.

Just as long as she was not responsible for anything going wrong this time too. Not that! Even if it meant staying on this side forever.

In the darkness, the antique clock ticked on the wall. Only the beating of her elderly heart responded. Had the smouldering candle not been so thin, and had Dafna's eyes served her better, she would have laid out the cards and foreseen the coming day in them.

Throughout her long life, her late mother had often said:

'The last half-kilo of coffee in the house was burned, as Dafna was coming into the world.'

The great lady had had a long and painful labour. Suppressing her screams, she had clenched her teeth so hard that it had made her left incisor crooked. Since then, whenever she laughed her lovely feminine laugh, whose sound adorned the light-filled house, it had seemed like a lost sign. As Dafna did, in that large, contented family with its good fortune, enough for at least three more generations.

The maid who had been roasting the coffee that morning was alarmed as she heard the ever more piercing screams reaching her from the big room, from the mother-to-be, her lovely mistress. She forgot herself, staring blankly at her helpless hands. When she was aroused by the smell of burning coffee beans, it was too late. Knowing that their

8

lovely mistress was sensitive to bad signs, someone tried to think up a more satisfactory explanation. But despite the fact that when her youngest daughter first showed the world her large eyes, that seemed clouded with a dull membrane, the last half-kilo of coffee in the noble house had burned, a good sign had after all carried the day: the song of a rare bird which sang three times from an early flowering cherry in the family's garden.

In the afternoon, as every day, the great gentleman had come back from town. A serving lad ran up before him with bags full of offerings and even two kilograms of coffee beans. The gentleman was informed that a little girl had been born. Loving his wife's beauty, he loved in advance the beauty of his female descendants. There were enough men in the household already.

Nevertheless, it happened! Although for a time everything was forgotten and that bad sign stayed out of sight.

But all of a sudden the lovely lady noticed that Dafna was ugly. She had already taken her revenge when she chose her name. The day after the birth, when they brought the silver mirror to her in bed (it is not appropriate on the first day and does not bring good luck), and she noticed the crooked tooth under her full upper lip, she knew. She had given birth to an unlucky child. She named her out of spite. Dafna! And she glowed with contended malice when everyone in the house listened, baffled, to the collision of the

9

two syllables in that strange name which was not to be found in any calendar.

When Dafna's first blunder occurred, followed by ever more frequent and serious ones, usually marked by the sound of the family's precious china breaking, her strange name acquired its special surname as well. Dafna was registered in the book of births under her family's surname, long and resonant. This surname recalled proud days. It was spoken at the long family table, accompanied by the clink of the family silver and the china with the gold trademark *Alt Wien*.

When the first piece shattered, when it cracked along the very centre of the gold trademark, the lovely lady's uncle remarked briefly, not out of ill-will, but rather in an inspiration left over from the days when he was a young man in Budapest and Vienna:

'*Pehfogl!*'

That is how Dafna acquired her special surname. It was given her in a word, the short and only word her handsome uncle had spoken, in the days when he still had youthful sideburns and fire in his eyes, like an extra in the last act of a Viennese play. There were already five dead bodies on the stage when he came on with a halberd in his right hand and announced in a booming voice:

'*Pehfogl!*'

This time with no halberd, with no lush sideburns or fire in his eyes, but in the same booming voice, he had stared at Dafna, still squinting in confusion at the ruined *Alt Wien* piece, and announced:

'*Pehfogl!*'

Everyone present had looked at Dafna. As in the solemn silence when the priest pronounces the name of a child. And they saw that her large eyes had lost their dull membrane, but they themselves remained flat and without depth. Not beautiful. Worthless, round tokens left over after a lost game.

Whether it was because of her eyes, or something else, Dafna remained unmarried. Her special surname became known even outside the house.

It was not that she did not have admirers. But they were always beneath the standards of the house. They did not measure up to the surname that took two intakes of breath to pronounce. When Dafna was approaching the age of an old maid, the great house agreed silently to lower its standards. At least until Dafna was married. In the meanwhile, time, and not just Dafna's unlucky influence, had deprived it of many of the signs of its former prosperity. There was still a long table with heavy chairs round it. But the very last piece of *Alt Wien* had gone, not this time due only to poor Dafna's butter-fingers.

So, it was decided that Dafna should marry. That a young man should come to the house, introduce himself and sit down. Everything would be done without a fuss unworthy of that house, all the more so since it was an old maid who was to marry.

Spring was already well advanced and the early cherry tree in the yard was bearing fruit. But the day had dawned cold and damp, straying by mischance into the calendar.

The household sat, Dafna sat and the young man, a bank clerk of low rank, sat. If his origin and surname were unworthy of the house, at least his brow was high and pale. His eyes were suitably shy. His fingers fine and long.

He took the cup of coffee graciously, although it bore no famous trademark. The minor bank clerk nodded his head politely. He said 'Yes, please!' And 'No, thank you', nicely. He did not blow on his hot coffee. He did not slurp. He drank exactly the appropriate sip. When he lowered his cup onto the tray in front of him it clinked just as in the days when the *Alt Wien* had clinked in the house. He took the sugared rose meekly without licking the little silver spoon. He made a nice arc with his hand before he placed the little spoon in the crystal glass from which he had taken a sip of water. After that he gave a quiet, noble sigh.

The members of the household gazed contentedly at the little silver spoon as at an exotic fish in an aquarium.

Just two or three more sighs and a nice full stop, worthy of the house, would have to have been placed on this scene. But it was just then that Dafna's eldest sister came into the room, the one most abundantly endowed with her mother's beauty. Here came the unpractised extra to confuse the order of images and scenes and wave a halberd at just the wrong moment.

The water in the glass became cloudy and the little silver spoon lost its sheen. The sister came in with the ill-humour of a former beauty. She looked somewhere over his pale brow and, with barely a greeting, asked:

'Whose is that *dreifirtl* on the hook?'

The end! Dafna no longer wanted to see the minor bank clerk nor was she able to answer the household's insistent persuasion and questions as to why. That *dreifirtl* just kept ringing in her ears. And the minor bank clerk appeared before her inner eye in a coat, which reached only three-quarters of its full length. As time went by, she was increasingly certain that on that ill-fated day, her sister-the-beauty had been carrying a halberd in her right hand, while down her pink cheek hung red sideburns, although admittedly not lush ones. When Dafna began to read cards, her sister-the-beauty appeared as the knave of hearts. Dafna forgot her long dead uncle who once, to earn some pocket money or for the love of a capricious actress, had been an extra in the last act of a theatrical performance.

So the modest book of expectation closed over the girlhood of Dafna Pehfogl and an old maid's cards were laid out on the table. Dafna learned to read signs in the cards and through them to reveal the coming days. A dark shadow was already sprouting on her upper lip. It was too late for marriage negotiations. That day the little silver spoon had fallen to the bottom of the crystal glass like an anchor dropped in vain. When the minor bank clerk left, and the heavy front door closed behind him, smaller now in his three-quarter coat, Dafna had drunk the remains of the tepid, tasteless water in the crystal glass. Later, in her clumsiness, she had broken the glass. All that was left her was the little silver spoon. Since that day, it had rested like a silent secret among the trifles from Dafna's girlhood.

Misfortunes of one kind and another continued to befall her. Even when the sound of the name *Alt Wien* had faded from the proud house. The worst had been the one with the electric coffee mill. Even now, the night before her crossing to the other side, when she thought of it, Dafna hastily clutched her left hand with her right.

She fell asleep just before dawn. She was roused by the ticking of the antique clock.

When the rigid frontier was set up between this side and that, and the only one of the family left here was Dafna, they had held an anxious consultation. The former beauty had said ill-temperedly:

'Out of all of us, it had to happen to her.'

14

The others said nothing, then someone sighed and murmured:

'Yes, *pehfogl!*'

But no plush curtain fell onto the stage. They did everything they could to bring Dafna over to their side.

At six-thirty, two young men with weapons and uniforms led Dafna to the bridge. One was tall, with a sharp nose from which a little drop hung. When the young man sniffed the little drop fell off, but was quickly replaced by a new, larger one.

'Damn autumn weather,' the tall lad swore.

The other one said nothing. He was small and dark. When she turned to him, just to try her luck, he looked at her irritably. And at her old-fashioned raincoat and little old-fashioned hat and flat eyes. Three yards away from the bridge, Dafna sensed the enemy and a bad sign. The knave of hearts had come up, although all this one had in his hand was a rifle.

They led her to the bridge and left her. The sneezing one gave her a push and hissed:

'Go on now, quick!'

Dafna stepped out as though in the large room where the children used to make living pictures during the winter holidays. She was always the one who practised longest and she was always the one who, sniffing, coughing or stumbling, spoiled the living tableau. But now she was on a bridge over which she had to move. The bridge between there and here. She clutched her little bag tightly to her.

She stepped boldly and decisively. Freed from other people's gaze and lengthy sighs. Her feet were light on the deserted bridge between there and here. She was already approaching the middle of the bridge and the other bank seemed quite close.

But, the time of the living tableau was not yet over and she felt a tickle in her nostrils. She had as fast as possible to bow, to make a charming curtsy, and garner the praise of the household.

Her heart was beating irregularly, although no longer in response to the sound of the antique clock. She could smell the aroma of burnt coffee in her nostrils. Had he come up behind her, she would have hurried and escaped him. But he was coming from the bank to which she was drawing near. That was where the gleam of the crooked incisor beneath the full lip was, and the golden trademark cracked through the centre, the ill-fated clink of long-ago china. Perhaps, if she hurried, she could anticipate the shattering of the fine trademark. Perhaps she could avoid the eyes of the man with the halberd in his hand who was watching her from behind.

She would turn round and curtsy. She would escape him. She was half-way across and she would try to appease her destiny. Maybe she would no longer be Pehfogl. A blunder – a matter of a fraction of a second and you pay for it for years.

She turned. She raised her left arm. (Of all of us, she had to be the only one who was left-handed, her sister-the-beauty used to say). The one who was looking askance at her had lost at cards the night before, he was as incensed as a hungry wild beast and was sniffing the air to catch the scent of bad luck. Dafna had not yet had time to smile. And the latest little drop had not yet slid off the nose of the one who was sneezing. And he waved his pistol.

'Why kill the old thing, you brute?" asked the taller one, beginning to sneeze repeatedly.

'Did you see the sign the old bat made!'

This time Dafna Pehfogl was fortunate in her misfortune. The bullet hit her in the heart. Perhaps she expired convinced that there was just a brief interval, a short pause before her life crossed from the unlucky to the happier track. In the big room, the children ended one living tableau and quickly arranged themselves to form another.

Dafna Pehfogl lay in the middle of the bridge. To the guards looking at her from each bank, she seemed like a large, strange bird hit by a stray bullet and there was no hunter to claim it.

They carried her over after a lengthy, difficult

procedure. The woman who was giving her the ritual wash, paused for a moment. Passing the wet sponge over the shrivelled old body, she came to the ring finger of the left hand, vulgarly crooked and stiff. Like the finger of a man trying to make a rude gesture.

'Whatever next,' muttered the woman who washed the dead and went on with her work.

No wedding ring had ever found its way to this finger, yet it, the second to last finger on Dafna Pehfogl's left hand, had found its way into an electric coffee grinder. That day in the big house one of her beautiful nieces was getting married. Wanting to be useful but avoiding glass and china, Dafna had offered to grind the coffee. As she held the electric mill in her right hand and pressed the red button with her thumb, her eye was caught by the pattern on a porcelain dish which someone had put down on the kitchen table. With her left hand she absentmindedly removed the lid of the grinder and in an instant, along with the half-ground coffee beans, her ring finger slipped inside the mill. She was taken to the clinic half-conscious in the car intended for the bride and groom.

The wedding somehow came to an end. The young couple left in a more modestly decorated car. After two years of bad marriage, the niece was divorced. Her sister-the-beauty said:

'Dafna was a *pehfogl* again.'

From that day, Dafna had a vulgarly bent finger on her left hand. When she was laying out cards, it looked like a strange ill-fated hook.

They buried her on a day that was, amazingly, quiet. No shots reached them from the other side. It was autumn, and the day bright and warm, as though it had strayed into the calendar. Family members wept over the freshly dug grave. The women sighed and pressed handkerchiefs to their noses and eyes. It was only on the way back from the cemetery that someone noticed that on the announcement of her death, from which her large flat eyes looked out, alongside her surname with the two in-breaths, instead of Dafna, it said Danfa.

'How can you expect people in this chaos not to get such a strange name wrong!' someone else responded.

They sat in the large room of the family house. They drank tea instead of coffee which had not been available for a long time, ever since the town was divided into there and here. After taking their first sip, they set their cups down on the tray together. They clinked in the old, long since forgotten way. And there was a special, solemn silence. Had anyone entered, they would have thought they were looking at a living tableau. Then there were two or three long sighs.

'Poor Pehfogl!'

Her sister-the-beauty glanced at the little bag lying

in the corner. The day before she had found the little silver spoon in it, an anchor left over from a long-since sunken ship. It was like the last act before the scene in which the extra with the halberd and bushy sideburns was supposed to rush in. A plush curtain hung over their heads.

And there was silence in the large room for a long time after that. As though in apprehension and evil foreboding. Who was the extra to look at now when he shouted *Pehfogl* in his booming voice? Now that the unfortunate Dafna bird had expired on the bridge between there and here?

GREETINGS FROM THE BESIEGED CITY

Thirteen for ten!

If twenty years had passed since that evening, rather than two, I would still have been certain that this was the offer he had chanted in his sing-song voice. He had a face that would have inspired titles such as *Boy in Blue, Boy with a Tear in his Eye, Boy with Rose* ... It was hard not to be sentimental about a face like that.

But we both recoil from such emotions. We know all too well how awkward one feels when they subside. Even on summer beaches we read serious books. When the sun's star paints the sky orange, purple, violet, red, one of the two of us says drily (we seem to take turns from one evening to the next, like conscientious watchmen):

'Well, have we had enough Greetings from the Adriatic?'

We mean the picture postcards of sunsets inscribed *Greetings from the Adriatic*. In the evenings tourists buy them at street stalls and send them inland, to cities where the asphalt is melted by the heat of summer and women's thin heels sink helplessly into it.

We don't buy postcards like that, even if, in the absence of any others, it means not writing to our friends and family at all. We did not succumb until that evening when we caught sight of those awful postcards in the hands of a boy standing at the beginning of the main street in Dubrovnik, near the Onofrio Fountain. He had arranged the thirteen cards, all identical, in two unequal fans. Cooling his flushed face with the larger one, he held out the other with the full length of his thin arm, like an outdated traffic signal. He was the *Boy with Postcards, Boy by the Onofrio Fountain. Boy at the Entrance to Dubrovnik. Boy Leading one into the First Temptation!*

In fact, there had already been similar temptations. Like the one to which I had ingloriously succumbed several months before. At that time, our little boy was already very good at distinguishing letters but he steadfastly refused to read. He would press up against me, thrust a favourite book into my hands and mutter:

'Read it!'

He maintained a dedicated silence. While I read aloud and my mouth grew dry, he would gaze calmly at a fixed point, without turning his head towards the book.

That spring before Dubrovnik (it was an unhealthy, sickly spring which instead of luring the buds out of the old trees, turned sensible people sentimental!), I had been reading him a little book by Paul-Jacques Bonzon, *The Seville*

22

Fan, a remnant of my own childhood reading. The original title was *L'Eventail de Seville*. Those were the first foreign words I had memorised, never having managed before that to reproduce the little Czech songs my father used to sing as he shaved. That was how he daily revived the language of his four-year bachelorhood in the country with the prettiest sound for the letter *c*. I remembered the French title of Bonzon's book because my romantic younger aunt, who had been born an old maid, used to come up to me while I was reading it, and ask, expressing her agreeable surprise each time by a movement of her eyebrows:

'Oh, so is my little fair-haired girl reading *L'Eventail de Seville*? Little fair-haired girls ought to read *L'Eventail de Seville*. *L'Eventail de Seville* ...'

She would lean over me and I would be suddenly overwhelmed by the scent of lavender and heather. I would close my eyes and whenever my aunt repeated *L'Eventail de Seville*, I would feel on my cheeks and eyelashes the caress of fresh air, as when you wave a fan briefly and rapidly in front of your face. Ever since then, when it is stuffy and oppressive (more under my skin than on it) I repeat two or three times in a half-whisper:

'*L'Eventail de Seville.*'

Oh God, will I manage it at the final and irrevocable ... at that moment when no earthly language any longer has power? When all fans are forever closed?

But, that question has nothing to do with the day when I was reading *The Seville Fan* to my son. If it has, it will be established without words. So, it happened that the now grown up, former little fair-haired girl was reading her son a book whose main character was called Pablo. The poor young man sold *orchito*, a kind of Spanish *boza*, a millet drink, and he fell in love, youthfully innocently, with Juanita who sold fans ... And so on, and so forth ... In the end Pablo dies. It happens! In books as in life. But you feel uncomfortable reading that to a boy who is listening to you, holding his breath angelically and staring at one spot, still believing someone else's eyes as they run over the printed pages of a book. But, does it not say in some important pedagogical material that, among other things, books accustom children to the fact of death? The lesson pales when it turns out that the child's parent must also accustom himself equally painfully to the child's getting used to death. On one occasion the parents of our boy (to avoid the sentimental 'we'!) had become heavily involved in such speculation when one of them cut the discussion short (hurrying to watch a football match on TV!):

'The best thing would be to give him that book *Death* by Vladimir Jankelevich. And in French, definitely. In the original. Then, before he gets used to death, he will get used to the French language. After that everything will be as smooth as milk ...'

That 'smooth as milk' isn't some foreign expression and the father of our child generally uses it when he's annoyed and when he means that everything is already going as it should and one should not blaspheme. And that matter of the book *Death* and Vladimir Jankelevich ... that's a response to the fact that the mother of our child studied comparative literature and still has a huge list of books whose titles contain the word *death*. Jankelevich's title is underlined in red. That means that the book is not translated into our language. It was written in French but, alas, after *L'Eventail de Seville* I never succeeded in learning more than a couple of hundred French words. Unfortunately, writers have not yet learned to write within such a restricted framework. That is why on my list Jankelevich's book is still a precious point of unexpended expectation.

Luckily (or not!), *The Seville Fan* was long ago translated into our language. But, what does that alleviation in the process of accustoming a child to death mean in the face of the fact that you are approaching the page on which the main character dies, and at the same time you can feel the incomparable warmth of your own child against your body.

To be brief and truthful... I confess that this time I succumbed. I suddenly decided to change the ending of the book. Off the top of my head, without previous preparation! It took quite a lot of presence of mind (not something that is taught in comparative literature courses) to prevent the boy noticing the change in the tempo of my reading and the uncertainty in my voice which was more a consequence of my being unaccustomed to lying than to improvisation.

And so Pablo succeeded in not dying, which he was, after all, not accustomed to. Because, when I exhaled and put the closed book down, in its printed pages he was still dead. As I was pronouncing the sentences that were not in the book, it seemed to me that, for the first time in our reading sessions, our boy turned his eyes away from their fixed point. He glanced suspiciously at the book then at my face. A pedagogue would say that he was beginning to get used to the fact that parents tell lies. Or that they become accustomed to sentiment!

I exhaled again in a manner more suited to a person to whom an injustice was being done than one who was in some way sinful. For the first time I thought with understanding of Otilija T., red-haired, intelligent and imaginative, but with a trace of unhealthy fever in her eyes. Many years had passed since we first met. We had known each other for only a short time: we were together in our first year at university and for just half of the second. But still, I remember her more vividly than any other person in our joint photograph at the degree ceremony. If it is my place to judge, the fact that Otilija abandoned her studies of comparative literature was fatefully stimulated by an event that took place in our second year, during the January exams, in the office of a tall, grey-haired professor. He was someone who, during his lectures, had enjoyed listening to the sound of his own voice which was one suited to a theatrical stage. He always

26

looked over our heads as though checking whether his voice was slipping too far away. He would pause and give a little cough, as though he were sitting on Greek Olympus at a time when the irascible gods lived there. And then he would start to speak theatrically again, but so as not to squander his precious voice.

There were five of us that day in his office. It was raining and a high, dead branch which the gardener had not managed to cut off during the spring pruning, kept knocking tediously against the window pane, buffeted by gusts of wind.

It was Otilija's turn to answer. She was somehow especially different. 'Like a snowflake on a summer's day', as that great Austrian writer whose books are an excellent weapon against shallow sentiment would say. Otilija was a special kind of snowflake. Ample, red-haired. But still, a snowflake on a summer's day, a red snowflake on a summer's day. She was unique. Simply a one-off. She was the unusual Otilija T. whom we had called Otikica from the first day. And she was just finishing her excellent answer. All at once the professor fell from his self-loving height into the shallows of a caustic intolerance. Later I realised that this happened to him when he felt that there was someone in front of him who might some day be able to stimulate far more scholarly fire than his cold voice and occasionally his barren pen had dispersed over the years.

The professor asked, just as that dry branch began beating against the glass again:

'And what was it, young lady, that happened to Anna Karenina in the end? Could you tell us?'

We did not know then that this question contained, in concentrated form, all his sterility and ineptitude. But, even if we had known, we would not have been able to comfort Otilija T. that day. She suddenly became a little island that was hard to reach from the mainland. Her complexion and her hair united in colour. The source of that colour, however, was not her hair but an unhealthy fever in her eyes. Her hair was quite innocent, regardless of the opinions of theoreticians who make a connection between the colour of a woman's hair and her character and temperament. Would my aunt, who used to recommend *The Seville Fan* to the readerly attention of a little fair-haired girl, have said:

' Oh, and little red-haired girls should read *L'Eventail de Seville* as well.'

No recommendation of any kind could reach Otilija T. She was a torch, and you cannot blow out a torch. In a voice that we did not recognise, with a verve displayed by unhappy characters who want to change the world, alone and isolated, she said:

'She married Vronsky. If I were a writer, every book would have a happy end!'

She did not become a writer, even after this announcement. She soon transferred to a different course, situated in a building where dry branches did not knock against the window pane.

She did well in her new course and found a good job. Books continued to have the kind of ends they have. On the whole unhappy, if one asked Otilija T.

She was lucky enough to find a job. But, that was not yet the end. For a while I lost sight of her and then I heard that she had had a baby. Unlike Anna Karenina, whose child, although born out of wedlock, knew that it was blessed by the love and body of Vronsky, of Otilija T.'s child no one could say who the father was. And Otilija T. was silent. In itself, that matter of a child and its father need not be a prescription for an unhappy end. But somehow Otilija T., whom I chanced to encounter in the street pushing a large pram, struck me that way. Like an unfortunate heroine pushing her burden towards the last page of the book.

There, by Onofrio's Fountain, I thought again of Otilija T. She would have been glad to receive a *Greetings from the Adriatic* postcard. Not because she had displayed a weakness for sunsets. Simply because the card contained an abundance of the red colour that Otilija T. had liked to choose for her clothes. The colour of her hair was a gift of nature, but it was not decisive in her choice of clothes. Women's magazines maintain that red hair and a complexion like Otilija T.'s look nicer with the colours of water and moss ... Otilija T.'s choices were largely guided by that fever let loose in her eyes.

We did not, of course, buy the postcards. When we had moved some way from the *Boy with Postcards*, we were suddenly overcome by a desire for ice-cream.

'The ones by Onofrio are best!'

That was spoken by our boy's father. His mother nodded in agreement. The boy was chasing an exhausted pigeon round Orlando's column. He had already forgotten Onofrio. When the father returned with three ice-creams, the mother opened her mouth to ask whether that boy was still there. But she desisted, realising sensibly that they would in any case be going back the same way. It was hardly worth disclosing her aroused sentiment for five minutes of unquenched curiosity.

The boy was sitting by the fountain. Now he was *Boy with Ice-Cream*. And he looked as contented as every boy licking an ice-cream did. *Boy with Ice-Cream* – that was an unusually striking image of innocent self-satisfaction. And, generally, everything there, between Orlando and Onofrio, was fine and noble.

It was only Otilija T., pushing her pram in front of her up there inland, who left a mournful track. The track of the pram imprinted in the melting asphalt was accompanied by the track of her heels. The track of the pram reminded one of abandoned tramlines. Beside them, one heel left a deeper mark, the other a shallower one. That was just the way Otilija T. walked. Stepping out more vigorously with one foot, in an inspiration stimulated by the fever in her eyes. With the other foot, it was as though she had changed her mind in mid-step.

In the autumn, when the first grey rains were falling and our summer suntan was fading, I discovered that the fever in Otilija T.'s eyes had been given a diagnosis. She went to hear it, when they took her away, after something terrible happened to her and her child.

She was sent to a hospital on the edge of the city, somewhere I never had reason to go. It is only when a city becomes a besieged city that you acquire a burning wish to reach its edges. Then you are drawn by a strong desire to step over the ring imposed on you by force. Then you gradually realise that there are always rings around you, albeit invisible and not always imposed malevolently. You cross them on those quite ordinary journeys the aim of which is a summer holiday or distance that may easily be attained by the simple purchase of a ticket. And all that interests you then is that edge of the town where such journeys start. Not remotely the one where sorrowful hospitals are built, in dead-end streets.

In the spring Otilija T. was back with her son. She was leading him by the hand now. When I met her like that for the first time, I greeted her, but she replied drily, not like that grey-haired professor, but like an automatic telephone answering machine:

'Would you remind me? With whom do I have the honour?'

31

I was taken aback and watched her as she walked away, without turning round. She was dragging the boy, just as red-haired as she was, determinedly. Even his clothes were red. In one hand, the one that was not clutched by a hand with nails painted with bright red polish, he was holding the end of a string at the other end of which hovered an overfilled pink balloon. It must have been Otilija T. who had blown it up. With all the strength of her lungs. It looked as though it was going to burst at any minute. Perhaps that was why I went on standing there for a while, watching Otilija T. There are some scenes that you simply must see. And not only scenes that affect you agreeably. Sometimes even unhappiness is seductive.

But the balloon did not burst. At least not as far as my eyes could see. They reached a distance sufficient for that sad scene to become an idyllic image. The distance wiped from my sight the chipped rim of polish on Otilija T.'s nails. And the runny nose typical of little boys there is no one to care for. And the rash in the corners of her lips which patients in the hospital at the edge of town usually have. When these details had vanished and it was no longer clear whether that child in the distance was a little boy or girl (did red suit it, then?), the distance granted me a pleasant picture. As though prescribed for a happy end. Two red heads, a pink balloon .. One head represented the other as maternally solicitous. And the other represented its own long-term prolongation on the endless path of parental reproduction. No, there was no sense in which one head was missing. The father's. It looked fine this

32

way. *Mother and Child with Pink Balloon*. A nice title! The unbearable summer heat had not begun and the asphalt was not melting and there was no mournful track left after Otilija T. and her child.

I soon forgot her again. Insofar as anything is ever forgotten.

A year later the city was surrounded and outside the ring that held it cruelly tight, there remained a few of its edges, in one of which was the hospital where Otilija T. was a patient. I never discovered where she happened to be at the decisive moment. Since she had a diagnosis that made her life an exchange of residence between there and here, I could only guess. It could have been both, because the rhythm of interchange was not predictable or regular. On the other hand, it would have been best if Otilija T. had finally found herself outside any story about here and there. Somewhere beyond the space of their painful interweaving. Somewhere where life unfolds like a light, sweet succession of themes, like a simple quadrille: *Boy with Rose, Mother and Child with pink balloon, Little Girl in Blue, Little Girl in Red* ... And so on – without end. A quadrille has no end. Either happy or unhappy.

But, empty desires aside, the city was surrounded and that, in itself, did not suggest a happy end. Red-hot balls were falling on the city. In an instant they transformed human bodies into bloody heaps of flesh. The most terrible thing, but unfortunately not the most infrequent, is when a

33

mother's shriek calls to her child as she stands over just such a heap. Then you wish that life was a book whose end was written by Otilija T. If Otilija T. is in the besieged city, then she is an island on an island. When you acquire the voice of an automatic answering machine, no one any longer expects you to get used to the fact that a living child can in an instant become a bloody little heap. You do not get used to the fact of death either, an ordinary one if there is such a thing, or to the page on which Anna Karenina throws herself under the train. If that is called madness, then I envy Otilija T. She calmed her madness in time. Domesticated it! Not waiting for it to be brought on by bloody little heaps of children's flesh. Otilija T. departed into madness in good time.

And what about us? We remained. Although for a few months after the city was surrounded we packed our two large suitcases. Not in order to leave the city but so as to take those few essential things down to the cellar, in case the flat went up in flames. In the besieged city, houses often burn floor by floor, usually from the roof down. Phosphorous bullets arrive from the other side of the ring. Perhaps those who fire them want to see an enormous blaze? Just as some people like to watch a sunset? Sometimes whole families disappear in that blaze along with their more or less trivial mementos. Perhaps even the occasional *Greetings from the Adriatic*.

A sunset does not damage even the fish swimming under the point where the sun falls into the sea. There, beyond the ring that is holding the besieged city in its grip, stands a man with eyes in the colour of which vile frogs could spawn. He gazes at the distant blaze, cools the barrel of his gun that has just fired the phosphorous bullet, and says to the man next to him (he does not have eyes, he has two snakes peering out of narrow slits):

'Well, enough firing for today?'

We took our suitcases down from the wardrobe in the bedroom. His suitcase and mine. Mine is older. I bought it in London after losing my old bag at a station. I don't know exactly in what part of the city I bought it, but I remember that at one point I was standing with it at Piccadilly Circus and looking into the face of a young man who said:

'You have beautiful hair! Are you going to Ireland?'

He had freckles and the English words he spoke were light, metallic. As there is no distinction between the formal and informal 'you' in English, I wasn't sure whether he was being insolent or not. I didn't take what he said about my hair as flattery. All the girls passing by me at that time had straight, greasy hair. Mine was a freshly washed mane.

Whether it would have been worth going to Ireland just for that, I don't know. But I sometimes regret that I have never been in that island-country.

The four letters on the metal plate on my suitcase disappeared long ago. My hair is still a freshly washed mane, even though it is hard to find water in the besieged city. While I was picking up notions about life from books, the image of sorrow imprinted itself in my consciousness like the image of cutting a woman's long hair. Sorrow came, but my hair was still long. Nevertheless, you retain some notions like charming little pictures in a young girl's pressed flower collection. The besieged city is an island and that is not an appropriate place for a pressed flower collection. Now Ireland is an ever more distant part of a whole continent that ships cannot reach. Perhaps another girl is standing at Piccadilly Circus with a new suitcase and a mane of hair. Someone approaches her and asks in a voice that forms words like light metal coins:

'You have beautiful hair. Are you going to the Besieged City?'

Since then the three little wheels have come off my suitcase. The boy pulls it along by its strap, shouting:

'Come on, little horse! Come on, you old nag!'

In my suitcase I keep things that no longer have a purpose in everyday life. The boy's outgrown clothes, old toys ... trifles with which I find it hard to part. When I travel (when I used to travel!) I empty the suitcase, look at the heap of things that falls out of it and reproach myself:

'Shouldn't these old things be in the cellar?'

His suitcase is more up-to-date, better preserved.

He travels (used to travel!) more often, so it has to be ready all the time. We don't put old things in it. He's the only one who can open and close it. The boy and I like watching. He stands over the suitcase and looks past it. He spreads his hands, and with his middle fingers presses little plastic catches on either side of the suitcase. The catches click, then with a little key that he keeps in a small sheath, he undoes the locks on the top. First one, then the other. The key turns a quarter circle. It clicks twice. He spreads his hands again and uses his thumbs to pull two little plastic tabs beside the locks. The suitcase becomes a large, open seashell. However often I watched him do it, I never succeeded in reproducing the same movements. Once, when he had to travel a long way away, to the north, I wanted to put something secretly into the suitcase which he would find when he reached his empty hotel room. Something to remind him of the boy and me. I didn't succeed. On the other hand, my failure simply saved me from what was, essentially, a sentimental gesture.

A fortnight later, a postcard arrived with a picture of a Finnish landscape and the message:

'Distance is amazing. I miss you both.'

The suitcases that were meant to travel to the cellar (in addition to journeys to the north, south, east and west, there is also a journey to the cellar), retained our old habits. Mine was still full of the things it contained throughout the year. Only the little book *The Seville Fan* was added. Our serious, important books stayed on the shelves. Many books

37

about death. But not *Death* by Vladimir Jankelevich which, in order to accustom you to the fact of death, still required a perfect knowledge of the French language.

We packed essential clothes in his suitcase, our degree certificates, photograph albums and documents. We put both suitcases in the hall and waited for days. In case fire came from the other side of the ring.

Soon the suitcases, standing there in the hall, began to be in our way. And we soon needed one essential little item, then another, then a third out of his. And to extract them we had to repeat the complex operation of opening and closing the leather seashell. We decided to empty it, to put everything back in its old place, and both suitcases (mine still full of old things) on top of the wardrobe in the bedroom. The good side of this undertaking was that *The Seville Fan* was at last beyond the reach of the boy's hands. He had begun by now to read books avidly by himself. He could easily have discovered the deception over the end of the story of the boy Pablo, It seemed to me, that if the book only came into the boy's hands, Pablo would leap out of it, papery and cut out like a silhouette. He would look at our boy and say:

'Your mother's an inveterate liar. I am incurably dead!'

Although you live in a besieged city in which dozens of people may die in one day from the blow of a single ball of

38

fire, you still find it difficult to start to accustom your boy to the fact of death. Which reading matter can you use for that? Although, when you compare the two planes, it becomes senseless. Our boy knows that a friend of his was killed a few months ago. A fragment of the red-hot metal that is let loose when the ball of fire bursts went through the very centre of his brain. The child's brain spilled onto the asphalt, before it had become familiar with the fact of death. And here we are, still protecting our boy from the fact that the hero of a book had died.

There are, however, facts that suggest a certain progress. Notably, I succeeded in opening his suitcase. I wanted to empty it, without waiting for him to come home. He used to stay out for a long time and I didn't want to burden him with trivialities that I could sort out myself in the meantime. It was only when I had opened the case that I remembered:

'But I don't know how to open it!'

But, it was too late. The seashell was already open. The jam-packed shell out of whose secret compartment (where he puts his documents and socks when he travels) fell a large envelope containing twelve postcards inscribed *Greetings from the Adriatic*.

If I am not mistaken (and I can't be mistaken), the *Boy with Postcards*, later the *Boy with Ice-Cream*, was offering thirteen for ten. Thirteen cards for ten dinars. He had gone back that evening for ice-cream in order to buy the postcards.

But where was the thirteenth card? The thirteenth *Greetings from the Adriatic*? So, he must have sent that postcard from Dubrovnik to someone, without my knowing. Karenina and Vronsky! The other way round this time! This did not promise a happy end.

In the besieged city everything is unusual but everything is at the same time ordinary. While people are dying nonsensically, I am caught up in a frivolous intrigue. The kind made for cheap novels. It's up to me to control it, this unexpected intrigue. I'll show him the postcards and ask drily:

'There were thirteen, if I'm not mistaken?'

That was what happened. But his reaction was unexpected. He did not even betray surprise: how come the postcards which had been hidden in the suitcase for two years were now suddenly in my hands?

'Yes, there were thirteen.'

'So where's the thirteenth?'

'I sent it.'

'Who to?'

'My parents. It means a lot to them in the summer. And they don't mind if the postcard has a sunset on it. They didn't study comparative literature.'

Our suitcases rest on top of the wardrobe. No one goes on summer holidays from the besieged city and no brightly coloured postcards reach it. Tracks still remain in the asphalt. Not only when the sun is baking. When it's piercingly cold as well, and red-hot balls fall, sent from the dark mountain by the man with frog-spawn instead of eyes, and a strange imprint is left in the asphalt. People call them roses. The besieged city is a horrifying rose-garden whose roses, after they bloom, frequently contain pools of blood. Once the boy and I came upon just such a fresh rose. He asked me quite calmly:

'Mummy, was there this much blood when Pablo was killed?'

'Which Pablo?'

'Pablo ... Juanita's. The one from *The Seville Fan*.'

That was exactly what he asked. There are some sentences that I remember for months, for years. Like those spoken in the office where the dead, unreachable, branch was knocking against the window pane. Like the offer at Onofrio's Fountain. Like the sentences I heard at Piccadilly Circus that had made me want to go to Ireland. Like the sentences that were full of sighs and smelled of lavender and heather. Like the realisation that distance was amazing. Like the terrible question:

'Would you remind me? With whom do I have the honour?'

41

It is time that I took them all, those fragments scattered over the years and different places, and arranged them all in a story. The reason came in a dream. Last night I dreamed about my younger aunt. It was cold, I kept trying to get close to her, but she kept pushing me away and when I started crying, at last she looked at me (she had quite different eyes from in real life and she did not smell of lavender and heather) and she said reproachfully:

'Could the little fair-haired girl find something to do? Auntie is translating *Death* by Vladimir Jankelevich.'

She sighed sadly and then glanced at her wristwatch (she never wore a wristwatch, but always a round watch on a chain round her neck!) and went on staring at the empty table in front of her.

I awoke with the feeling that I was suffocating and this time I did not murmur *L'Eventail de Seville*. I opened the window and breathed rapidly.

Sometime around midday I looked for my old notebooks and papers and among them that list of titles containing the word 'death'. The red line with which I marked the books which were not translated into our language had faded under *Death* by Vladimir Jankelevich.

There was just a little red line under *Jan* and a red dot under *h*.

If it were possible to summon a dream, I would have

summoned the one I dreamed last night. Let it come again. Then I would turn on a telephone answering machine in my voice and say to my aunt:

'Would you remind me? With which title, with which subject do I have the honour?'

I am hurrying to finish telling the story. It has to have a happy end. Otilija T. deserves that.

If only I knew what a happy end was! Did I know once and have forgotten? Like Anna Karenina whom Tolstoy finally allowed not to jump under a train. And now she is standing on the platform … standing, standing, standing … and what next?

It is a sunny afternoon and I shall conjure up, as in a spiritualist séance, the little picture of *Mother and Child with Pink Balloon*. Two red-haired heads, a pink balloon, hand in hand… but then what? Then what!

THE SECRET OF KASPAR HAUSER

That side came for this one, after all.

The two sides had parted as long ago as the day when the little dwarf, with eyes which seemed composed of narrow concentric circles, had been standing by the window at the end of the empty room. He tapped his hand with his ruler, looking nowhere in particular, and said:

'The bedroom goes on the north side!'

He had been sent by the architects' office recommended to us for the alterations to the apartment. I don't remember whether he said anything other than that sentence. I don't even know whether he introduced himself when we met. It sometimes seems to me that I just found him that day standing by the window. It is hard to be sure of directions in an unfamiliar space, especially when it is full of the traces of another, a stranger's life. It seems more important to satisfy your urge to remove the wallpaper with its torn strips and irregular bubbles. The traces of a stranger's touch were imprinted in the cracked, yellowing varnish on the doors. On the window panes, like the tiny stars of some long since extinguished galaxy, there were the left-over specks of flies from a long-ago summer. Around the bath plug were strands of someone else's hair. In the washbasin there was a sodden fag end with traces of violet lipstick on it. It looked like a TB patient's spittle. The worm-eaten parquet creaked as though under someone else's feet. In the bathroom, beside the lavatory, there was a crumpled newspaper with an old date on it and a large yellow stain all over the headline 'Caribbean volcano erupts'.

But, before I put on rubber gloves and picked up the strands of hair, the cigarette end and the old newspaper, I learned that the bedroom had to be on the north side. Was that an established rule that architects respected? Although this one reminded me more of an old clown standing on the stage of an empty auditorium smacking his hand in a vain effort to summon applause. He never reappeared. He vanished after carefully recording something in a tiny notebook and peering into every corner of the apartment. I was just beginning to think that he was looking for something in the wormholes, when he made a little bow and moved towards the front door. I nearly responded by clapping. He scuttled down the stairs in a manner unsuited even to an old clown, let alone an architect who had been recommended by a reputable firm.

I had not even had a chance to offer him the coffee I had brought in a thermos flask. I drank it myself. Three plastic cups full of unsweetened coffee. The glass jar of sugar had tipped over. I drank small mouthfuls of the hot liquid, staring at the little heap of sugar crystals scattered over the floor of the room that had from that moment become the bedroom. The room that faced north. For the first time in our new apartment, I felt weary.

We telephoned the office again and again a hurried woman's voice asked curtly for our address, and dictated the date and hour when we could expect an architect.

This time he was tall, with opaque, grey eyes, bent at the waist as though from a permanent stomach ache. He did not mention the north, or any other side of the world. He talked about surfaces, cubic space, insulation, a partition wall, laminated parquet, floor joists. These words acted like an antiseptic in that space filled with anonymous wormholes. He sighed loudly, as though wearied by what he was saying or surprised by the effect of his words. His breath lifted a thin lock of hair from his perspiring brow.

After that, many workmen passed through the apartment and finally our things moved in and a tablecloth appeared for the first time on our table. It turned out that the bedroom was indeed the one in which the dwarf with the concentric circles instead of eyes had tapped his ruler on his hand. I wanted to mention this at breakfast, but I was afraid that while I talked old wormholes might start to appear under the fresh white layers of paint.

As well as facing north, the windows of our bedroom also look onto a hospital. We are separated from it by the width of a road, two narrow pavements and the hospital park enclosed by a low green fence. The park used to have tidily mown grass, rose bushes which flowered every month and rare, exotic trees whose sumptuous flowers were replaced in midsummer by fruits of even more sumptuous appearance. They are inedible, perhaps even poisonous. They sometimes attract the longing gaze of the quiet child. They say that some diseases float, like exotic fruit, in jars of formalin in secret hospital larders.

In the mornings, I used to gaze at the hospital trees. I brushed my hair by the bedroom window. I swept it backwards with one movement and it fell over my shoulders. The trees shifted benignly away again.

We are separated from the other side of the street by its tranquillity. The only people who used to pass by lived in the neighbourhood. Occasionally someone who did not know his way around the city ended up here. Such a person would keep stopping and looking around. On Sundays, at noon, silent visitors gathered in front of the hospital gate with offerings for the patients. When the gate opened and the visitors disappeared through it, I realised that I had been witness to a disappearance. And I was just as helpless as those who disappeared. Yet they did return, in small groups or individually. Some of them turned and waved in the direction of the hospital windows. A shadow passed behind the lowered blinds.

Occasionally ambulances sped along the street. Their sirens rent the silence. Then the piercing sound subsided and silence closed in again like water over the drowned.

On sunny days, the street reminded one of transparent sea shallows in which the spine of a slender fish flashes, like a silver exclamation mark.

Parallel with this street, some hundred yards away, runs the city's main street. Cars once sped there, electric trams clanged. The inhabitants of the city hurried loudly by. As it passed over the shady courtyards and old-fashioned façades, the noise was transformed into the sounds of an aquarium.

There are no curtains on the windows of our bedroom. The room is filled all day long with the shade of the north side. In the morning, our eyes are not hurt by the sharp light of the rising sun. In the evening we are not concerned that someone might be watching us from the hospital as we move about the room lit by electric light. The blinds are down over there. Besides, patients have their own inner windows and they lean over them as over their illness.

Sometimes, before I fall asleep, I remember the dwarf, the way you remember a stranger who knocked on your door and asked you to look after some trifle for him for a while. He promised he would come and fetch it. Time passes and he does not come.

What he left does not take up much space or demand attention. But, as time goes by, the germ of someone else's secret settles in it. At any moment it can come to rest definitively on your tiredness.

If I were to tell him now about the dwarf, the bedroom and the north side, it would seem like an inappropriate confession. All the more so since I would be quoting someone who had seemed like a failed clown. Although, with clowns, I respect their reasons for sadness. But why mention such reasons over breakfast?

He would look at me enquiringly and sternly. And say that left-over stories should be thrown out with the morning rubbish.

In the evening I would pack up the refuse that accumulated during the day. I put it in a black plastic bag beside the front door. He left the house first. He dashed down the steps with the bag. He didn't so much as glance at it. Still without looking at the bag of rubbish, he hurled it, with an energetic swing of his arm, into the metal skip. He glanced towards our window and waved to me. Then he crossed back to this side of the street, I didn't know whether his reasons were the same as mine. I have avoided the other side since the day we moved into the new apartment.

On this side, exactly opposite the hospital gate, was a shop selling fruit and vegetables. The large window was full of boxes of oranges and lemons. There was never any seasonal fruit. Customers came only on Sundays when they were visiting patients and bringing them offerings. Then they were served by a girl with narrow green eyes. When there were no customers, she sat and read. Once it happened that she caught sight of me as I was passing with plastic bags

50

full of succulent produce purchased in the colourful market. She closed her book, looking first at my bags then at my face. She looked at me as if I was an enemy. The calculations and reasons had yet to be established.

But, life was still order that had not yet begun to disintegrate. It lay in drawers with folded white bed linen and little bags of dried lavender. It was still all-of-a-piece, even if it was sometimes disrupted in the morning by the disagreeable sound of the alarm-clock. On one such morning the north-facing room acquired a new secret. I woke up before dawn in order to take an antibiotic. Replacing the bottle from which I had tipped a red and yellow tablet onto my hand, I caught sight of a bright, swaying blot that I had never seen in this room before. It was trembling on the spine of the large book I had been reading the previous evening. That is how I discovered that in the early morning a little ray of sunlight manages to penetrate into the room that faces north.

I didn't tell him about this either, when he woke up. Remedies sometimes lose their beneficial effect when you pronounce their name.

We wake up too late or else that rare ray of sunlight penetrates into our room too early. But on that day, when I put on my rubber gloves, I had believed that it was enough to remove all the traces of strangers from our new apartment so that nothing would catch us off guard.

Nevertheless, over breakfast, he noticed something

51

unusual in my face. With the tip of his knife he spread a layer of butter over his piece of toast and said:

'Has something happened?'

At that moment the glass sugar bowl I was reaching for tipped over. But that happened to me regularly, almost every morning. I brushed the sugar that had spilled onto the tablecloth onto my hand, carefully and patiently, every last tiny crystal. I shook it out into the sink, turned on the tap and watched the jet of cold water wash the remaining crystals from my hand. Dissolving in the water, the sugar disappeared down the waste pipe.

'Are you sweetening the river again?'

Every time I did this, he asked me the same thing. I didn't reply. I drank my unsweetened tea. The taste of the tea in the warm liquid is stronger that way. In the perfect layer of butter in front of him there were already traces of his teeth. When we finished breakfast, I hurried to clear the remnants from the table. I washed the china cups, the spoons and knives. Once, we had been staying with the Konrads. When we came back, I wrote on a piece of paper torn out of the boy's notebook:

'What was on the table at the Konrads? Five coffee cups. With dried brown dregs in them. Three large glasses with various patterns round their rim. In one of them were the crusty dregs of yoghurt. A blue and white box of Gingavil-C, biological gel for massaging the gums, made by Galenik, 15 grams. An open packet of little sticks for cleaning the ears. One little stick outside the packet. Unused. A newspaper. A headline: "Double Dilemma". A half-completed crossword. In blue ball-point. The word "picado" written in green. A cat.'

The piece of paper lay for a long time beside the telephone , where we leave little notes and messages. In a different-coloured pen, but I believe in the same hand, down the length of the piece of paper was written: The Secret of Kaspar Hauser.

Perhaps he had wanted to remind me that there was a film of that title showing. In that case he would usually have noted the time it would be screened with three exclamation marks. But after the words 'The Secret of Kaspar Hauser' there wasn't even a full-stop. Just a tiny, washed out orange blot. Perhaps the scrap of paper would have gone on lying beside the telephone for a long time had he not noticed it one afternoon when he was repeatedly, but unsuccessfully trying to get through to some important number. Between two attempts he glanced at the piece of paper and asked:

'Is this a shopping list? Is it done with?'

He crumpled the piece of paper and threw it into an ashtray. It vanished with the cigarette ends into the black plastic rubbish bag. The next morning he dashed down the steps, and it was already too late to ask him. I watched from the window as he threw the bag into the skip. And drew back before he was able to glance up in my direction.

Some months later, a colleague at the editorial office, doing a crossword over a morning coffee, asked:

'Who was Kaspar Hauser?'

'Hauser turned up in Nuremberg in 1828, saying hardly more than a few words, unable to write anything apart from his name, and eating nothing but bread, drinking nothing but water. At first it was assumed he was a tramp, and then he was thrown into gaol and became an attraction for scholars ... '

'Come on, your coffee's getting cold ... Did you have an encyclopaedia for breakfast? And what's the name of that green fruit which ... '

I didn't reply. Just as I had not replied that morning to the question:

'Has something happened?'

The question mark at the end of his question had slipped away while I was engaged in my daily ritual with the spilled sugar. When I came back to the table, he was already bending over the dish of boiled eggs. He chose the smallest and tapped its end with a little silver spoon. When he did this he neither saw nor heard me. Maybe since the day the boy had asked us:

'Are there boiled chicks in boiled eggs?'

The city is surrounded and things have begun to vanish, the precious props of our mornings. The little silver spoon remains but eggs and nicely packaged tea-bags have disappeared. Sometimes, in the place where the brightly-coloured market used to be, I find two or three eggs. I pay a lot, as much as all twelve little silver spoons had cost. I keep the eggs for the boy. Before he eats them boiled, he draws on the top of each of them with a coloured pencil. He does not mention the chick, but still, while he eats the egg, he has a regretful expression on his face.

The glass bowl remains, but with no sugar in it.

'What we need now is that sweetened river you worked on so assiduously for months.'

There is no water in the tap either. We fetch water from another part of town and bring it back in plastic containers. When that source dries up, we look for a new tap in some other part of the city. The door of the shop where the girl with the narrow green eyes used to sit is broken and its frame swings when the wind blows or shells fall. Inside it is empty apart from occasional stray dogs and street cats.

The boy rarely goes out now. A thousand and one dangers lie in wait for children in the besieged city. He stands by the bedroom window, gazing longingly at the hospital garden. The exotic trees still flower and make fruit. If you bit into them, they would take over your blood supply. Perhaps you would then shrink and be able to fit into a jar of formalin. In a besieged city it is not bad to rest in the secret cool of a hospital larder. When you wake up, you become a secret, a riddle, an attraction for scholars.

They take the wounded to the hospital. Sometimes they are only bloody trunks with no arms or legs. And yet, everything still seems remote. Painful, but remote.

And then that side came for this one. He was injured somewhere in the main street. They took him to the hospital, cleaned and dressed his wound. He arrived in the evening. In the hospital they told him that the wound was half an inch away from where it could have been fatal. Whoever said this must have been tapping his spectacles against his palm as he spoke. He needed to take antibiotics but in the besieged city there were none, not even for the seriously hurt.

He fell asleep lying on his side. So as to protect the wounded place. He moaned dully and sorrowfully. I did not manage to fall asleep until just before dawn. I woke half an hour later and found him lying on his back, so that he was pressing on the wound. Not only was he no longer moaning, it seemed as though he was not even breathing any more. His face was tranquil and distant as though he was on his way somewhere where there was no room for anyone apart from himself. And he was so close that I was touching his side.

If I looked in the other direction, perhaps I'd delay

his departure, I thought. The green book with silver letters was lying over there, and on its spine was that trembling blot of light I had seen once before. If I was quick and quiet, perhaps I'd catch it.

I know that light is not sensitive to touch or sound. But still, I edged towards it as though it were a live butterfly. I lowered my hand onto the spine of the green book and now the blot was trembling on the back of my hand, like a transparent, asymmetric butterfly. Turning my palm up, I moved back to the bed. I knelt on one knee, supporting myself my other leg, as though I no longer had any strength in my arms. I pushed him with my free hand and when the place on his pyjamas which covered the wound came into view, I carefully laid the hand that had touched the light against it. I pushed him hard and succeeded in turning him onto his side. He woke up.

'What on earth are you doing?'

'I'm seeing whether it hurts.'

'And ... does it?'

That morning we breakfasted on thin slices of bread spread with a barely perceptible layer of margarine. We drank, both of us this time, unsweetened tea, or rather tepid water into which we had lowered a tea bag which had already been used several times. If such tea was spilled on the tablecloth it left no trace. Just dampness that dried quickly.

'While they were cleaning and dressing my wound yesterday, I looked at our bedroom windows. Exactly opposite. ... I saw you go in and out of the room twice. You opened the wardrobe. It seemed as though you were cold, very cold. You wrapped yourself in something. '

'And ... was I cold?'

We looked at each other across the table. We leaned our elbows on its surface, with our hands forming goblets, we held our little china cups at the level of our mouths. Now, now I'd tell him why our bedroom faced north. And I'd tell him about the little ray of light that this morning had spared me a few fractions of a second of his departure.

'Do you know why our bedroom faces north?'

I tapped a little silver spoon against the palm of my hand and in the cup that he had put down I saw concentric circles that reminded me of somebody's eyes.

'Does it?'

He plunged his spoon into the tea. In the colourless liquid without a single sugar crystal, it looked like a hook cast there with no hope of success. Somewhere far away there must have been that great river, where all the tiny crystals from my palm had ended up.

I put my cup down too. Now there was a silver hook in it as well. When we looked at each other across the

58

table again, the question marks had slipped away from our questions. Before the boy woke up I'd remove the crumbs from the tablecloth and shake them onto the window sill where the birds landed. I'd put away the cups and spoons. All that would be left would be the white tablecloth that I spread over the table every morning and put jealously away after breakfast. This time there would not even be a trace of spilled tea on it. If the two of us were to disappear at this moment, if a large wave were to wash over us, if a volcano we were unaware of were unexpectedly to erupt, and if some time, a hundred years later, someone were to discover under its cooled deposits the traces of our former life, nothing would be written down. Nothing could be counted and listed down under the question: What was on the table?

And yet, even on blank paper, it was always possible to write with any kind of pen, without even a question mark, exclamation mark or full stop:

The secret of Kaspar Hauser

In Nuremberg, the clerk of the Great Council had placed two dots after these words. One above the other, as though anticipating a list. Then the clerk had raised his pen from the paper. He held his pen solemnly at the level of his chest, ready to lower it in an instant. He waited. He waited! He waited for the honoured gentlemen, with scalpels in their hands, to complete their important work. They were looking for the answer in Kaspar Hauser's open skull, after he had been violently killed.

59

The brain in front of them looked like a cauliflower drenched in blood. Or an enormous walnut in raspberry juice. Or ... just like every other brain they had ever had under their hands and scalpels.

But in this one they were looking for an answer. They were looking for something different, special. Something that would be an explanation. Something that would explain the secret tormenting them.

The clerk could already feel his hand growing numb in the air. But, solemn and conscientious, he continued to hold his pen ready and listen for what the gentlemen would say.

But in the end the wise men laid down their bloody scalpels. They wiped their hands on linen cloths. One of them thought that the blood on his hands was somehow particularly greasy.

The clerk was still ready and those three words were waiting for a list.

But the serious members of the Great Council simply shook their heads thoughtfully. The scribe was already supporting his numb hand with the other.

There was nothing there!

THIRST IN NUMBER NINE

'Christ is born!'

I knew it! I had guessed it. Just as I had felt for days, for months, as I passed this shabby, grey door, that a face with blue eyes lived behind it.

I never knocked on it. Nor on any door in this entrance, apart from the one in the basement. On that one there was a large plastic name plate bearing the inscription CARETAKER in flowery lettering.

In the doorway: the caretaker and his three children, as though they had always been there and would be forever. One on the father's left. Two on the right. If the father were to step away and the children move closer together, each would come up to the next one's ear or eyebrow.

The smallest one, on the left, was holding onto his father's trousers with one hand. In the other he had a piece of dry cake. It was unusually large, fatefully large.

As I greeted the caretaker and shyly introduced myself, the tiny face behind the large piece of cake was already clenched in a painful mask.

'If I have understood correctly ...'

I did not manage to hear the caretaker's question to the end, already quite overcome with anxiety. Might the child choke? It quickly put down the remaining piece of cake, gave a sad sigh and began to hiccup. Whenever I opened my mouth to say something, it hiccupped. My throat was dry. As though suddenly and irrevocably all the tiny, delicate folds of mucus had straightened out, forming a painful, tight membrane. If it went on, the mucus might have leapt right out. Like the taut, transparent bubble that appears when you cut into fresh fish. But I had no fins. Just helplessly dangling hands and in one of them, in my clenched, sweaty fist, the piece of paper I was supposed to give to the caretaker. The paper confirmed that new tenants had moved into staircase number nine: the holder of residence rights with two members of his household. Under the seven short, typed sentences, there were two signatures in blue and a stamp. But the caretaker was thorough and slow. He scrutinised the form attentively, and then, as though comparing something, studied my face, arms, legs. He spoke solemnly while the smallest child pressed itself still more firmly against his trousers.

During this time, the second child was indifferently munching the remaining piece of cake. Again a painful spasm and hiccups. Then it was the third child's turn. It chewed calmly and indifferently. The sound that came from the depths of its chest was the loudest in this newly formed trio. The youngest child looked sternly at me. Were they expecting something from me? And I had knocked on the door quite unprepared!

62

The father coughed. Just as solemnly as he had spoken. He was holding my sheet of paper in one hand, in the other a grey folder. He told me that it was extremely nice (… and very timely…) that the arrival of the new tenants had coincided with a time when important decisions were to be made about entrance number nine. The tenants' council in number nine had decided to react energetically to the frequent, unwelcome visits of unknown and irresponsible nocturnal passers-by. They would often come into this entrance, and here the caretaker coughed painfully and, leaning confidingly towards me (I could see that his dry cheeks were touched with pink), he whispered: to urinate. He had himself proposed that a new lock be bought and keys issued to all the tenants. Entrance number nine would be locked at night. The proposal had already been voted on and the new tenants had simply to agree … or … perhaps they wouldn't?! The flushed cheeks of the proposer turned pale and his lips trembled. His voice betrayed his potential disappointment.

'It's up to you to decide whether to participate in the realisation of the unanimous decision of the tenants in entrance number nine!'

There was no more cake. All three children stared at me as their father solemnly handed me a pencil and sheet of paper resting on a piece of firm cardboard. I signed my name under the text of the decision of the tenants of number nine. Just to get away as soon as possible from the increasingly infectious trio! There was not a single crumb of that fateful cake left. In the depths of my chest I felt a slight ache. I could not remember where and when I had felt it before.

As I mounted the steps in long strides, two at a time, I remembered that children should not be given dry cake without a mouthful of milk. I had read that somewhere. If I could find it, perhaps it was a newspaper cutting, I could knock on that door and reproach the neglectful father. Would he appear again with all three children?

Oh, those new faces that peer out of unknown doorways! My eccentric uncle, who liked to stroke the tip of the moustache on the left of his mouth (he had none on the right), used to say:

'New faces are like false lures. You don't want to look at them. But you can't stop yourself. The impulse surfaces in any case! Plop!'

I reached the top floor out of breath, hastily unlocked the door, and soon felt the agreeable cool of the kitchen floor tiles under my feet. I opened the door of the fridge, but all I found was a half-empty plastic bottle of oil. At least there was water in the tap, as I might have recalled had this been a quite ordinary thirst. But I was looking for a carton of milk in the fridge. A blue and white carton with the expiry date printed on it. This time I would not have looked demandingly at the date. Would my hand know how to make that short, precise cut with a knife through one of the top corners of the carton?

'Thirst is a higher form of hunger,' my left-whiskered uncle used to say.

I stared at the white inside of the fridge lit by a tiny gleaming light and knew that I was going to think of the eccentric family virtually every day.

'Whoever you think of first in a new home, he'll be in your thoughts forever!'

He said that too. Sucking his left-hand whiskers.

Him again!

Nevertheless, tranquil days and months followed. And there were no new faces. Nor false lures. Nor did I knock on any more strange doors. The figure of my left-whiskered uncle settled into my memory. And my thirst was quite ordinary.

In keeping with the unanimous decision of the tenants of number nine, we were given little keys for the lock on the main door. We began to get used to our new apartment, the fridge was full, and a long period set in at number nine without any new, important decisions being made.

We got used to the order of the different coloured front doors, to the smells and sounds by which we distinguished each floor even with our eyes closed. Meagre signs of the lives of the tenants of number nine became familiar. I forgot the hiccupping trio. Just occasionally, in passing, I would hear children's voices and laughter from behind the door in the basement. And their father's coughing! The caretaker of number nine must have been thinking up a new, important decision.

Entrance number nine became an ordinary habit. Like a brief limbering-up exercise before entering the apartment that smelled of menthol. The length of time between two sounds and that smell depended on how tired we were and the speed of our steps.

On the first floor was the sound of a sewing machine. A metal bee working tirelessly. Opposite was a door from which music could be heard. Someone's hand sliding over the radio dial. On the second floor was a brass plate with large, thick loops on the letter 'B'. It was fixed onto a door behind which a man's and a woman's voices could be heard. Her voice was strong and it would repeat the same sentence several times. When it stopped, the man's voice would say:

'Don't shout. I can hear you. And shut the door. There's a draught. Dear God, does no one in this house ever listen to me?'

From opposite came the sounds of a kitchen. Strangely, there were no smells. Just the clinking of enamel, china, cutlery ...

On the third floor there were no sounds. From the door on the right came the aroma of fresh bread, sometimes of cinnamon and vanilla. Opposite was a door concealing something that stank of hospitals. Sometimes I would deliberately pass closer to it. I felt a piercing heat in the nape of my neck and hastened up the next stairs. I rushed into our apartment, but for a time I went on feeling a slight prickle on my nape.

On the fourth floor something scratched at the door. Whining, barking. When the door opened a boy and a dog appeared. The boy chased the dog down the steps. He looked round only when he reached the next landing and mumbled in a rush:

' 'afternoon!'

Opposite was silence. The quietest door in entrance number nine. With no smells I could recognise. This was not the silence of an empty apartment. Nor the kind that reigned in apartments crammed with old, heavy furniture. I must be able to identify it! That special, secret silence.

Perhaps one should put one's ear to a door like that. Or the metal end of a stethoscope. Can one listen to an apartment as one does to the depths of a human chest?

But that is not what I did. Just as I was always afraid to put my hand into the breast of a plucked chicken and, with one, swift, abrupt movement, pull out all that was left: the blue heart.

Soon the shabby door began to reveal itself through a colour. It appeared in the little glass pane through which one could peer from inside. Like a light, blue shadow. And that is how it was day after day. So that I began to think that someone with blue eyes, hidden and secretive, was watching me from inside. Watching me as I climbed to the top floor with my heart beating ever more rapidly in my chest.

It was not a child. It would have betrayed itself by laughter or some other sound. But the blue-eyed door remained perfectly silent. Inside, there was someone leaning on it, someone accustomed to long, patient waiting. Someone who no longer measured time.

An old man? An old woman? Lonely old women often peered out like that. Hardly anyone ever knocked on their doors.

My game with the blue began. I would stop by the door and raise my hand as though waving to someone. Then I would drop it suddenly towards my head and arrange my hair. The blue soundlessly disappeared.

Or else I would smile. I'd look at the blue. The way I sometimes smiled at old people sitting on benches in the park. Then the blue would stay framed in the circle of glass. Not giving itself away by the slightest sound.

It happened that I would set out absent-mindedly, particularly on mornings when the day was like cold water that one had to step into. Then I would go straight past the blue-eyed door, but I'd quickly remember and stop. I would think of going back. I felt that without the blue my day was deprived of a beginning.

'A day without a beginning, a day without an end!'

Ah, that was my left-whiskered uncle speaking, again!

But I liked the end of the day. I liked the shady peace of the top floor and the smell of menthol. Towards evening, it was stronger and caressed my dry nostrils benignly. It would be terrible if the day had no end, while in my chest, from the depths, something unknown and troubling was beginning to grow.

Sometimes I would think: perhaps the blue has gone.

Then I sighed with relief: it was there!

But what if the door should open? I had not anticipated that.

Then it happened.

Before the blue revealed itself in two little eyes with thin, pale lashes and a captive tear, the person who had been watching me silently and constantly for months made herself known by her unusual, Russian name.

A Russian woman in number nine.

The sound of her name came permeated with three-part hiccupping. Together the caretaker's three children announced:

'Daddy sends kind regards to the new tenants. He asks you to be so kind as to sign here. The tenants' council is discussing the purchase of a new rubbish bin and a broom for sweeping the steps.'

'A yellow bin!'

The voice of the middle child came first. The youngest followed:

'The old bin's fallen to bits! So has the broom!'

The oldest child coughed painfully. They were standing side by side, each up to the next one's ear. They were looking at me and I felt a pain in the depths of my chest.

The familiar three-part sound began again. But there was no cake. They must already have eaten it as they knocked on door after door. And it must always have been a piece of the same cake. Dry cakes last for a long time and don't easily go mouldy. By the third floor, the caretaker's three children, bearers of the important decision of the tenants of number nine, had devoured the last crumb of the piece they had broken off. All that was left was the terrible three-part sound.

'Under Auntie Galina,' said the oldest child, handing me the pencil, paper and piece of firm cardboard it was resting on.

'Auntie Galina Nikolaevna,' added the middle child while the youngest nodded obligingly.

And so I signed underneath Galina Nikolaevna's long, illegible signature. As I did so, I felt an increasingly strong pain in my chest and I thought that I ought to give the children a mouthful of milk each. There were at least five blue and white cartons with a freshly imprinted date on them in the fridge. But how could I offer milk to someone else's children? They would tell their father. It would be suspicious, insulting.

The caretaker's three children went away, hiccupping. They would tell their father that the decision had been unanimously signed. He would write it out in his formal hand. He would stick the piece of paper up on the notice board by the main entrance. And the name of Galina Nikolaevna remained in our flat together with the sound of hiccupping. Like a face seen in a broken mirror. Carried over into the sound of a broken music machine.

'When you move into a building where a Russian woman lives, that's where you're meant to await old age.'

That's what my eccentric uncle used to say. After his death, he left two thick notebooks filled with nonsensical sayings like that. And they kept occurring to me ever since we moved into entrance number nine. In the family we used to whisper that a Russian woman had eaten the right-hand of his moustache, choked and died. And that afterwards my uncle had abandoned his rule of growing old in a house where a Russian woman lived. He experienced old age and death (which was not something my left-moustached uncle liked to mention) in a house in which no single Russian woman had ever lived or ever choked to death in due to her craving for a man's right-hand moustache.

Those who visited him before his death were mostly silent, listening to his tireless voice and strange nonsense. After all, my left-moustached uncle was interesting to listen to.

In fact, someone maintained that my uncle used to shave off his right-hand moustache every day. He used his right hand to make important gestures. He had no time left for such silliness as twisting his moustache. But his left hand and his left-hand moustache –that was another matter!

In entrance number nine, I had not yet experienced old age (my uncle did not like to mention death) but I did experience the first big explosion that rocked the city that soon afterwards became besieged.

All the doors opened at almost exactly the same moment and the tenants rushed down to the cellar. Terrible noises drive a person into the depths, even smelly, damp ones like the cellar in entrance number nine.

Under the only bulb in the cellar, feeble and flickering, I caught sight of two small blue eyes and knew: that must be her! Galina Nikolaevna!

One of her eyes was smaller than the other. Had it shrunk from peering through the tiny glass circle? From her other eye a captive tear threatened to fall at any minute. From long waiting it had become an opaque, dense drop, inappropriate for a blue eye, even if it was an old person's. In front of me was a thin, nondescript little old lady, unlike the attractive sound of her name. In a satin housecoat with light blue and green roses printed on its brown background. Under the cellar light that swayed from the strength of the explosion, Galina Nikolaevna's eyes looked like two worn, fake emeralds. A sad, aniline imitation. They could not possibly have been the eyes of those mysterious Russian women from the long, romantic novels that girls read in the daylight, by a half-open window.

She had put on an ugly grey waistcoat over her dress. Galina Nikolaevna! My first Russian woman. Women like her certainly did not possess an expensive trunk in which they brought, all the way from Russia, a beautiful ball-dress with a long, excessively long train, long enough for many new, extravagant ball-dresses to be sewn from it year after year. When the train was all used up the Russian woman would die, in deep old age. All that would be left was the ball-dress brought from Russia. The Russian woman would be buried wearing it.

But, all this is just some crazy fairy tale, or, perhaps, one of my eccentric uncle's pieces of nonsense. No, he never said that or recorded it in either of those two notebooks.

But he said enough, and talked in such a way, that here I was in the damp, dark cellar, searching for an empty page in an invisible notebook. Had my uncle made it all up? His left-hand moustache was quite real!

Fine questions for a night when red-hot balls were falling onto the besieged city. My throat was dry. I heard a child's scream. The boy said:

'Mummy, I'm thirsty.'

So, this was it. What was meant to happen. You went down into the cellar, you felt desperately thirsty while upstairs, above you, in the fridge, inaccessible, were plenty of cartons full of milk. Plenty of jars of fruit juice. In this cellar there were only a terrible thirst and an ugly satin dress.

Never to climb up to the menthol and the blue and white cartons. A dog whined in the dark corner. The Russian woman was standing under a light-bulb, whispering:

'But why ... why ...'

Her voice sounded as though she had just arrived from Russia. And she had already used up the long train. And even the dress.

Ten days later she knocked at our door. In the meantime the telephones had stopped working in the besieged city. All of them except those with a combination of digits like our number. Galina Nikolaevna had somehow discovered that in entrance number nine, the new tenants' telephone was working. She rang her son who lived in another part of the city.

'Kolya, Kolya ...'

She repeated that name softly, for a long time, and then replaced the receiver helplessly. She thanked us and thrust a withered apple which she took out of the pocket of that terrible satin dress into the boy's hand.

Afterwards, she began to drop in. Occasionally and briefly. There was always the telephone and 'Kolya ... Kolya ...'. And always before she left, saying 'Thank you so very much' (I think she once said 'spasiba'), she would thrust something into the boy's hand. A sweet, chewing gum, a little piece of chocolate ... Once, in the boy's hand, after 'Kolya, Kolya ...', there was a shiny ornament used to decorate New Year and Christmas trees. And it was summer, the first summer in the besieged city. Just as hot as the fiery balls that were falling onto the town. For a time the boy used the ornament, looking at his face in its shiny surface, and then, once, without meaning to, he trod on it. The ornament turned into hundreds of tiny, shining splinters. He collected them in his child's spade and said:

'New Year's won't come. It's over!'

Galina Nikolaevna's meagre pocket soon dried up. She used to put her hand into it out of habit, and bring it

75

out empty. She looked at me helplessly and said:

'Do you know that over there, in Russia, I had two aunts, both called Agdofia?'

That day Galina Nikolaevna left us, like a token with which one pays for telephone calls, the little story of the two sisters, both called Agdofia.

Over there, in Russia, a long way away and a long time ago, a woman gave birth to a little girl. And they took the little girl to church to be christened. The priest stood beside the still nameless child, bent over her tiny face, shook his shaggy head and began to chant in a resounding voice:

'I name thee Agdofia!'

Some years later, the same mother gave birth to another girl child. She too was taken to the same little church to be christened. And the same shaggy head bent over the little wrinkled, pink face and his voice rang out:

'I name thee Agdofia!'

One of the household coughed timidly and whispered into the ear of the shaggy head:

'We already have one in the house!'

Unruffled and not looking at the speaker, the head pronounced in its resounding voice:

'Let there be one more!'

Somewhere around the time when she bequeathed us the story of the two Agdofias, Galina Nikolaevna stopped knocking at our door. For days an old invoice lay on my desk with 'Two Agdofias' written on the back of it.

The first terrible winter in the besieged city began. It arrived early, during the autumn months. The heaps of snow were as high and heavy as the ones Galina Nikolaevna remembered from her childhood. And there was no power or fuel. Parquet was used for firewood throughout the city including entrance number nine. Old paper was burned. Furniture. Books. Someone even burned the only tree in the courtyard without seeking the unanimous approval of all the tenants in number nine. Besides, the caretaker had already abandoned the besieged city, with all three of his children. That was at the time when it was still possible to leave the besieged city. Soon a terrible, impenetrable ring was drawn tightly round it which could hardly be overcome by adults, let alone children, especially if there were three, each those reaching the other's ear. All the important, unanimous decisions vanished from the notice board in entrance number nine. The smell of vanilla and cinnamon vanished. What was left was the smell of a clinic. Behind the door with the large loops on the letter 'B', only the man's voice could be heard:

'Did you say something?'

There was no woman's voice.

There was no dog either, or boy with it. The remaining tenants met as they hurried past. They were living through their first terrible winter in the besieged city. They warmed themselves by tepid stoves. In one such stove, in our flat, the old 'Two Agdofias' invoice burned. In the besieged city old invoices cease to be valid. Their value is not enhanced even by the traces of strange little stories jotted on the back of them. But still, while the 'Two Agdofias' were burning, it seemed to me that the flame was licking something similar to one of those two notebooks belonging to my left-moustached uncle. But I soon stopped thinking of him. There was nothing to conjure up any of his strange, silly sentences in the terrible days we were living through in the surrounded city. There remained only a pain in the chest and the thought that the train of every ball-gown, no matter how long and luxurious, would have burned up long ago in Galina Nikolaevna's stove, as she struggled unsuccessfully with this vicious winter. Besides, Galina Nikolaevna had not brought a ball gown with a long train with her from Russia. Everything about her was ordinary, even wretched. Apart from her voice and the captive tear.

She began coming again. Usually towards evening. For no reason. She would sit for a few minutes, say nothing, rub her frozen hands and lean confidentially towards me:

'The telephones ... they're not working, are they?'

She no longer put her hands into her pockets. Nor did she leave us little stories like that of the two Agdofias. She

78

began to ask questions. Soft enquiries.

'And do you know what's in store for us ... what's in store for us wretched people?'

Her tear was still captive and it seemed to me that it was devouring the blue of her eye from within. As though one of Galina Nikolaevna's eyes was no longer blue! There was something dull and diluted in it. Something sad, inexpressibly sad. If that captive tear were to slip down her old woman's cheek, it seemed to me that Galina Nikolaevna would have been quiet and reasonable again.

But the tear did not slip. And Galina Nikolaevna asked questions. Nonsensical questions.

'Do you have any milk?'

Looking absently, in no particular direction, she whispered:

'Keep your milk, you poor people! You'll soon be needing it!'

There is no milk, of the liquid kind. The last carton disappeared long ago. We sometimes get powdered milk. I keep it jealously for the boy. For a glass of milk a day.

And why was it milk she asked me about? It was always the same! Always that milk! And that nonsensical warning in her voice.

Now she was standing in front of me in the cold morning. She had heard my footsteps and come out to meet me. She was wearing that satin dress again. She had wrapped a thin grey blanket round her. She was shivering, squinting and whispering by the half-open door.

'Christ is born? For you too?'

I looked at her helplessly. I felt that pain in my chest again. Like a frequent, sharp twinge. Something moved from the depths to the surface, following the spasm. Now, finally, I recognised this pain. I had first felt it ten years ago when I held my left breast to the tiny lips of my newborn boy.

Galina Nikolaevna did not know that the previous night I had been dreaming of sounds. Like frozen birds falling out of their nest. And what did that have to do with her Christ, who had chosen such a bad time to be born? Why now?

Galina Nikolaevna looked at me sadly. That foolish game with the blue had ceased long ago. This was something serious and difficult. I looked at the old lady, then at my hands and chest. Like an unwilling new mother, unprepared to take her newborn child. What to feed it with?

'He's born, he's born ... Auntie Galina ...'

I ran down the steps afraid that the captive tear might reach me. It seemed to me that Galina's eye was giving up and the tear was finally beginning to slip. I ran along the street. Without stopping for breath and without feeling tired. I ran right to the editorial office. In the doorway, I said to the colleague who had spent the night there:

'Christ is born!'

I wanted to address that frozen, sleepy man properly, but I could not remember his name. He was rubbing his stiff hands, looking at the death notices scattered over the desk and, without looking round, he replied:

'Does anyone care about being born this morning?'

Someone else came in. From the next-door room where there was a fire smouldering in a tin stove. I smiled and said:

'Christ is born!'

He looked at me wearily. He pointed at the papers that had arrived on the editor's desk during the night and responded in a half-whisper:

'Really born?'

Then the three of us fell silent. The one whose name I couldn't remember was tapping his pencil on one of the death notices. The other rubbed his knees, looked at us and said:

'A low or a high start? Low or high?'

He went out of the room without waiting for an answer to the question I did not in any case understand.

Judging by the expression on the other man's face, he was not thinking of replying either. He went on tapping his pencil.

I leafed through the papers on the desk, and the warmth that had accumulated in my body as I ran from home drained out through my fingers. I rubbed my hands, one against the other. On the piece of paper I picked up, it said:

'The famous ballet dancer Rudolf Nureyev died yesterday in Paris, at the age of fifty -three.'

'Nureyev has died!'

'Who would think of dying now?'

I turned round to see whether there was anyone else in the room. Just the man whose name I couldn't remember. On my way to the little office toilet, I caught sight of the notice board and a note that someone had pinned there a few days earlier.

'Any citizens or medical establishments that have the epilepsy drug UDANFEN are asked to take some urgently to the porter at the RTV nursing home for S. Dugarić.'

The previous day, someone had stuck a little picture of a cartoon character across the top left-hand corner of the mirror in the toilet. With big pink ears and a sticking out violet tongue. When the city was not surrounded, pictures like these used to be packed and sold with chewing gum.

Children collected them and stuck them into albums. The filled album was sent to the sweet factory and then, a fortnight later, a packet full of chocolate, sweets and chewing gum would arrive. It seemed to me that it was this very picture that the boy needed to complete his album. Picture number twenty-nine. I still remembered. If I could partly lift the picture off the mirror, I would find the number on the back. Under the creature with the pink ears and violet tongue someone had written in blue felt-tip across the whole width of the mirror: antimation! There was no woman in the editorial office in the habit of writing in lipstick on mirrors. But there was a young man from the sports' page, with a large mole beside his right eye, who sometimes left messages like this on the mirror in the toilet. The day before, on the cultural page, a text had been published which said that in the besieged city we were living in *a pure post-Disney world*. Before they left the printer, the last sentences had run: *The final act is the mercy of the shell, that ultimately radical tool in the process of decomposing the world. In its wake, not even the proverbially all-powerful animation can put things back together again.* At the printer's the letter 't' had been added to 'animation' and the signatory of the text, when she opened the paper, found *proverbially all-powerful antimation.* The news spread through the office like a catastrophic fire. The culmination was when the young man from Sport, choosing a moment when the agitated author of the fateful text was in the room, asked the colleague next to him quite seriously:

'What was the name of the character in that

antimated film ...?'

Witnesses of the scene maintain that the huge spectacles worn by the *heroine of culture*, a sign of her 'proverbially all-powerful cool' began to weep with fury.

The pink character was still sticking his violet tongue out at me. I kept looking at it. I was grateful to the hand that had put it there. And to that mischievous boy from Sport. His letters flickered in front of my eyes. The violet tongue gave extra strength to their colour. They helped me not to lower my eyes.

I would not lower them. Not even to the level of my own reflection that was somewhere there, out of range of my direct gaze. I felt a pain in my chest. A current, which had started in the depths of my breast, was finally reaching the surface, reaching the two burning spots from which at any moment thin, tepid trickles would start to drip.

I would not lower my gaze. Nor would I touch the material of my clothes to feel whether they really were damp at the level of my breasts. Sometimes, for important but inexpressible reasons, you have to believe your body, and not just your eyes.

HOW WE KILLED THE SAILOR

1.

If I mentioned it, he'd say I was being petty and that was unworthy of me. He'd close his eyes and, as though he were speaking about someone who wasn't in the room, he'd say:

'I'll count to three to make it go away. There, she didn't say a thing. One, two three. Forgotten!'

That's what he did when I pointed out that he was spreading the margarine too thickly on his slices of bread; when I remarked that he had given away almost the entire contents of the package of humanitarian supplies that the inhabitants of the besieged city occasionally receive. All he'd left us was a little packet of green mints. I once told him they reminded me of my grandmother who had died long ago – my mother's blue-eyed mother who was never hungry. It's true that we still had the cardboard packing. It burns well, but we won't use it. The inscription on it and the list of contents may one day feed some future story.

He closed his eyes and counted to three when he noticed ... but I won't say what. Maybe I'll use that too, when the shame passes, to feed some bitter story. For the time being, let it be forgotten.

The room had lost its box-shape. The light of the thin candle didn't reach its corners. It created a dim, uneven oval that shifted lazily if an unexpected current of air happened to touch its tiny wick. There was a transparent, trembling film over us. The few objects that were bathed in dim light, and the two of us, made up the inside of a giant amoeba. We were its organs, pulsating in the same rhythm, but not touching. Is an 'amoeba' that single-celled organism covered by a transparent membrane we looked at down the school microscope? If you touched the drop of water it was floating in with the tip of a needle, it would slowly curl up. Right now in the besieged city, where tonight no fiery balls are falling and no whistling bullets are being fired from the other side of the encircling ring, there are thousands of membranes hovering like this. The people in these bubbles of light are silent. Frightened, tired or indifferent, they are silent. Or listening. Hoping for sleep. To overwhelm them and spare them this vigil.

He had lit five cigarettes that evening and each time he used a new match. He put the dead match down in the saucer by the candle. In the ashtray lay cigarette butts and the narrow red band from the cigarette packet.

'Why are you doing that?'

I sensed that sleep wouldn't come for a long time yet. But, as I uttered the question I was aware that it was unworthy.

86

He didn't reply.

Now I had a reason to be angry and speak.

'Why are you doing that?'

I didn't care what was worthy of me and what wasn't. He looked at me and waved his hand, as though removing invisible headphones from his ears. He'd put them down for a moment and focus on me and my impatience.

'Doing ... what?'

'Using matches to light your cigarettes!'

'What am I supposed to use?'

Now he was prepared to put his invisible headphones properly away. He was interested in learning something new, something he hadn't heard before. He was expecting me to tell him where the sun could rise apart from in the east. That someone was killed every day on his daily route through town, that he already knew.

'The candle! You know yourself that we don't have enough matches. They're hard to find. The candle's alight, so use it for your cigarettes.'

There were already too many words in our silent bubble. Added together and expressed like this, they were all unworthy. Without them, we would just have been two organs pulsating to the same rhythm until they were overcome by sleep.

He looked at me as though he was standing in front of a stupid child who understood nothing and who had to have everything painstakingly explained to it.

'I can't!'

'You can't ... what?'

'Light cigarettes with a candle!'

'Why not?'

'Every time a person does that, someone dies somewhere in the world.'

If he had said this in daylight, or had there been a light bulb burning in the room, I would have laughed. I like it when a room is lit up like an operating theatre. I would even have remembered some images from films in which He lit cigarettes from the candle illuminating a dinner for two. First for Her, then for Himself. Gazing the whole time into Her eyes while the audience sighed deeply in the dark, in unison.

Besides, whatever he did, at least one person died somewhere in the world every second. There were even cold statistics about that. In the books that the candlelight didn't reach. That was why, suddenly and unexpectedly, his answer put me under an obligation, like a holy rule whispered into the ear of an unwilling novice.

2.

Maybe one day I'll scatter all those matches into his hand and say:

'That's how many people you've saved from dying!'

Then red-hot balls will no longer be falling on the besieged city and people in it will not die from tiny pieces of hot iron in their bodies. They will again die of illness and old-age. There will be light bulbs again and no one will be obliged to light cigarettes from candles. That will only happen in films.

I've been collecting the dedicated matches for three days now. I put them into an empty Solea cream tin with 'contents: 250g' written on it. But even if it didn't, I can assume from its size that it can hold another hundred or so matches. Sometimes I miss one and it ends up in the ashtray. In the morning I dig it out from under the butts. After that, the tips of my forefinger and thumb stink all day and the child frowns when I touch the end of his nose.

The matches he lays beside the saucer with the candle don't stink. There is even something agreeable about the slightly piquant smell from the phosphorous tip that remains even after it's extinguished. When I take the lid off the tin and count the matches, I'm aware only of the left-over smell of the cream. It is sweetish, like a woman's deodorised armpit in summer. Huddling in them, resting, are the souls that have been saved. There are twenty-five of them for now. When I close the tin, they come to life. I listen in to the sounds they make while the tin rests on my hand. Twenty-five saved souls rest in my hand. Today in the besieged city fifteen people were killed by one fiery ball (sent from the dark hill where the bad people went). No one had wanted to save them. I'll see their faces tomorrow in the newspaper obituaries. What about these saved souls in my hand? How old are they? What are their faces like? How much good is there in them? Do they know that there is a besieged city somewhere in the world with the saviours of their souls in it?

3.

I found out where this idea of the candle and the cigarettes came from. The morning was quiet, but as though damned. At such times I reach frantically for the books on the shelves. I open them, leaf through them, put them down. An old bill fell out of one of them. On the page it slipped out of, in the last line, it said that every time you light a cigarette from a candle, somewhere in the world a sailor dies. This was a book by Dario, our former neighbour. He smoked a lot, lighting each cigarette from the last. Now Dario is somewhere out there in the wide world. And the sailors are in a harbour, somewhere on the sea, in a ship, in a tavern, in the bought embrace of some lady of the harbour ... Are there any sailors where Dario is living now? On the other hand, if you were to thrust that sentence published long ago back at its author,

90

perhaps he would not remember that he had written it.

Like in that film ... was it called 'Night'? A man and a woman come out of a house after a long, barren night that has made them strangers. They sit down on the grass. Dawn is breaking. She takes an old letter out of her handbag. She reads it aloud. Emphasising every sentence. Declarations of love, words of tenderness, swearing devotion till eternity ... When she has folded the letter, she puts it back in her bag and looks enquiringly at the man. He asks:

'Who wrote that to you?'

'You!'

Dario's 'somewhere in the world' is now America. Everyone has his own troubles, even if he isn't in a besieged city. But he doesn't have to think about matches and candles. He can switch on ten light bulbs and turn the room into a dazzling operating theatre with no dim corners nibbling at the space, where painful questions nest. He lights his cigarettes with a lighter. The first one in the morning with a lighter, and then through the day, each one from the last. When he uses up his lighter, or loses it, he buys a new one. He can choose a new colour and trademark every time. And he's left the all sailors' souls to us. He has off-loaded all their weight onto our weary souls that even sleep no longer spares.

'Do you know Dario's address in America?'

'Which Dario?'

91

'The writer Dario, Dario the writer.'

'The writer? No, I don't. Why do you need it?'

'No reason.'

4.

This morning I put only three matches in the tin. All three stink of old ash. There's still room in the tin. When I toss it from one hand to the other, I hear cheerful sounds, the sounds of tiny souls sliding and bumping into each other. They are enjoying their loss of weight. Yesterday, when he saw me playing with the tin, the boy said:

'You're a child now. You've got a rattle. A really ugly one!'

Now I have to find a second tin. Until I find a better one, I'll use the box that once held long, thick matches with yellow phosphorous tips. It says 'Budapest' on it. I was there once, but I don't remember the building in the picture. It isn't ugly. But it wouldn't be worth going back there to see it.

This box won't last long. It's already worn at the edges. For the moment, there's a little ball of paraffin wax resting in it.

While we sit beside the candle, he makes three or four of them in the course of an evening. He collects the dripping wax with his fingers. The hot touch can't be enough to burn him, but it's quite enough to make the chilly room feel cosier. Some of the wax slides onto the saucer. He forms a little ball from what remains between his fingers, with the tips of his thumb and forefinger. When it's half-formed, he puts it on his palm and rolls it with the forefinger of his other hand. Taking my arm, he holds it by the wrist and drops the little ball into the palm of my hand, it's quite cold now and smooth. There's no trace even of the short-lived warmth it picked up from his palm.

He touches the little ball in my hand with his forefinger again. Now I feel the touch of his fingertip as well as the slight tickle of the little wax ball. In the morning I collect the little balls from the table and place them in a glass jar with the words *Kompot švetsky* on the label. There's a picture of two blue plums under the first word. When I have collected a lot of little balls, I melt them into a narrow candle.

But this morning I also placed one wax ball in the box with Budapest written on it. That's when it happened!

Nothing particular preceded it. It had been an ordinary day. He came home late. Not looking particularly tired. That silent membrane already covered the room. At around midnight he took a cigarette out of the half-empty packet, then put it to his lips, but before he had separated one lip from the other, he made the face people make when their nose is itching and their hands are full. He moved his lower jaw upwards and his lips moved towards the tip of his

93

nose. His upper lip, comically pinched, touched his nose. Nothing special.

I don't remember a single film scene where an actor did that before killing someone.

He reached for the candle with his right hand. He raised it, on its saucer, to which it was secured by a broad wax base. The saucer has a picture of a rococo lady in three colours on it. Grey, violet, gold. The lady is sitting on a swing and a long arc separates her from the young gallant who has, presumably, just pushed her away and is now waiting for her to come back. The wax base of the candle covered part of the picture. Part of the lady's face was hidden. You could see her wig, with its comic curls. And the lady's legs. They are painted violet and grey. Her feet are separated from one another and have little narrow shoes strutting on them. The little golden shoes of a rococo lady. When the picture is completely revealed and daylight reaches into the room everything looks somehow different. Deprived of colour and action.

The candle in his hand was raised to the tip of the cigarette. A trickle of wax ran down the thin stalk out of the hollow round the wick. It covered the lady's left leg. For a time the leg could be made out under the little transparent pool of paraffin, until it cooled, solidified and became an opaque blot. Musing on the lady's leg, I forgot the sailor standing on the deck of a ship sailing from one continent to another. He was pressing tobacco into a pipe with his broad thumb. He had

94

turned his back to the wind. Did he strike a match? He raised it to his pipe. And fell. As though struck down. As when one player's pawn knocks out his opponent's and it is no longer in his way.

5.

He is smoking. He was away for three days and two nights. In the besieged city men have duties that keep them out of the house a lot. Should I tell him that the night before he left he killed a sailor? I'll tell him. I'll tell him tomorrow:

'Put out your hands. Palms up.'

I'll put the tin on his left hand, and the box that once held long matches on his right hand. I'll step away and say:

'Those are the souls you've saved and one you didn't.'

Will he feel their different weight?

My God, in these giant amoebas, in their silent membranes, words and games acquire a weight that should be forgotten with the morning.

'Give me a cigarette!'

'Since when have you smoked?'

'Since this evening ....'

He taps the packet lightly and a cigarette slides

out of it. I take it with the fingers of my right hand, with my left I lift up the saucer with the candle. A trickle of wax runs down the thin candle and in an instant the rococo lady's other leg disappears as well. Just the tip of one little shoe peers out, no bigger than the sharp end of a needle.

The lady is completely smothered by the wax base. Besides, her smiling gallant who is waiting for her to come back to him in an arc on the swing ... There, he's vanished. Their coquettish game has been stilled by the hard pool of wax.

Now we are tranquil. For a moment at least. I inhale the cigarette smoke inexpertly and cough. There are no more sailors whose lives and souls depend on our tiny actions and decisions, weariness and forgetfulness. There are no more ladies and gallants whose game is in our hands. Just the two of us, alone, waiting for sleep. Today more people died in the besieged city. Perhaps their names and pictures in the obituaries will one day feed some future story. Like wax which you shape into a little ball and when it cools, drop onto someone's open hand.

I shan't throw away those two boxes. I shan't empty them. I'll leave them somewhere, in one of the dark corners that gnaw at the square shape of the room. When this is all once again brilliantly lit up one day, shall I find them?

Shall I ask:

'Who left this here?'

Shall I be able to say:

'I did!'

DEATH IN THE MUSEUM OF MODERN ART

'How would you like to die?'

'What do you mean ... how?'

'That's what's written here.'

'Die?'

He had put the *Times Atlas of World History* under the paper on which he was noting my answers. We use it when we write at night. The boy likes leafing through it when the shells fall.

He waited for me to reply, looking at my hand resting in my lap. It reminded him, he had said the day before, of a tiny baby. Its nappy changed, dressed, and peaceful. On the little table between us lay a photograph of me. Taken in front of the ruins of the old hospital. The reporters who come to the besieged city like taking pictures of ruins. The hand I write with was still unharmed then but I had thrust it deep into my pocket. I had drawn in my neck and hunched my shoulders, as though I was cold or uncomfortable. It seemed that I was stepping out of the photograph. Or should one say: stepping down?

'So, how would you like to die?'

He was hurrying me with someone else's questions, like a waiter or a shop assistant serving an indecisive customer. All that was missing was 'madam'. The questions had reached me a fortnight earlier. I put off answering them, day after day. In the meantime, there was this problem with my hand. (That's why he had to write my answers for me. He had given his own in ten days earlier).

Another ninety-eight inhabitants of the besieged city had received questionnaires like this. Before they came to the question *How would you like to die?* they were asked what happiness is, what they feared, where they would like to live...

This reminded me of the little confession notebooks in which young girls and boys used to write, the aim being to encourage those questioned to confess who they were in love with. But here, they were not asking who you were in love with, but – how you would like ... wish ... to die.

The answers, illustrated with our photographs, would be published in a luxurious magazine with shiny covers. Part of the edition would be kept in the Museum of Modern Art in New York.

What did they want of us? Something like those doctors who spill two or three drops of ink onto a sheet of paper and ask their patients:

'What does this blot remind you of? What do you see in it?'

'Nothing!'

'What do you mean ... nothing?'

'I don't see anything!'

'They're not asking you what you see or don't see, but how you would like ... or wish, to die. Here, translate it yourself the way you want!'

He knew how awkward I felt with shop assistants and now he was deliberately imitating the way they spoke in order to hurry me up. In my wardrobe there was a pair of shoes I had never worn, except when I was trying them on in the shop, four years ago. As I stood in front of the mirror, I glimpsed the expression of the assistant who was promoting me into a person on whose decision the fate of children in an orphanage depended. She had large glasses, worn high, at the very top of her nose. Their lenses did not look as though they were correcting anything, but like two windowpanes, recently washed. Twins peered bad-temperedly out from behind them.

'Well, madam, have we decided? I have other customers waiting!'

'At Kristina Verček's!'

'Kristina who?'

Men did not read the column that had been appearing for years in the local paper, every Tuesday. Kristina Verček, a qualified cosmetician, part-time lecturer at the College of Cosmetics, was the favourite reading matter of my women colleagues at the editorial office. I used to read *Pearls of my Cosmetics* infrequently and without interest, until I noticed the same sentence in three consecutive texts.

'It is a well-known fact that we all want to live for a long time, no one wants to grow old.'

The copy editor had once changed the verb 'to grow old' into 'to get older', but I was eagerly awaiting the fourth text for quite different reasons.

This time the expected sentence came between the address *My dear readers* and the advice that *One spoonful of oat flakes, previously ground in a coffee-grinder …* Whether the linguistic adjustment had been made in that one key sentence or not, I did not notice. I don't remember having noticed. What I was expecting, and what I received, was an invitation!

On Friday I had done everything I could to ensure that the editorial board would put me down to work on Monday, as that was the day the porter brought the pink envelope with Kristina Verček 's text in it. In fact, I did not have to try hard at all as my colleague was delighted to accept the swap. She intended to use it to prolong her weekend from which she said, licking her lips as she thanked me, she would *bring me something sweeeeet …. sweeeet! Delectable!*

On Monday I sat in the empty office and responded to the invitation intended only for me. I crossed out the word 'grow old' with correcting fluid. The open pink envelope lay on the desk smelling of the pungent tinctures that I had liked looking at as a child, touching the glass bottles in which they were kept; there in the artificial light of the laboratory, a room without a single window, where my father had taken me after repeated and persistent pleas. How his severity and the cold expression of his face were transformed in there! A magician's working mask. But, my father did not make cosmetic tinctures; he oversaw the mixtures and colours in the production of porcelain. But still I did not let myself be distracted by the smell of the pink envelope. The correcting fluid was already dry and over the blot under which the word 'grow old' lay I wrote in black ballpoint the word 'die'. I did not feel like a copy-editor making linguistic adjustments but neither was I like a thief with a curious area of interest. In a half-whisper, I repeated the word 'die' the way my father, bending over his tinctures, used to whisper formulae kept in books with a strange, pungent smell.

The only response to my voice was the steady hum of the press from the depths, behind concrete partitions and walls. This time it was not mixed with the murmur of voices from neighbouring rooms. It continued in my ears even when the office joker came in through the abruptly opened door, with all the force of his bulky body and asked in a booming voice:

103

'Are you writing something ... delectable? Something sweeeet?'

The next day, the telephone in the editorial office rang at 8.30 am. At that time the only people there were those who were trying to avoid some domestic 'troublet' (the bulky joker's word) or those who, like me on this occasion, were expecting an important call.

On the line, of course, was the voice of the qualified cosmetician, part-time lecturer at the College of Cosmetics and the valued contributor to a local paper with a tradition of nurturing cosmetic subjects – all this was contained in the voice of Kristina Verček. I immediately apologised in the name of the editorial board and explained that the mistake must have crept in at the printer's. But she spoke as though calling for a quite different reason. In her soprano voice she dictated what type of skin I had; warned me, in a mature female alto, about bags under the eyes, and finally, in an indisputable baritone, she ended:

'So, I'm expecting you tomorrow, then. At exactly six p.m. You've remembered the address? Take care, I'm on the fourth floor and the light on the stairs doesn't work.'

My 'yes' did not manage to overtake the metal 'click' in the receiver.

I reached the door, where a little fluorescent plate gleamed with the words 'Qual. cosmetician, K. Verček' on it, up a long, dark staircase, twice hesitating and ready to give up, not to respond to the invitation. The person who opened the door had a pronounced, dark moustache.

It was not long ago that she had given her readers as many as three pieces of advice on how to rid a fuzzy female face of hair. But the whiskers of the part-time lecturer at the College of Cosmetics did not strike me as in the category of a cobbler's worn shoes. Those fine whiskers reminded me of some female characters (my friend the writer who says that he does not see but hears faces, maintains that characters do not exist). I was thinking of the characters of a writer whose name I could not remember. They often had whiskers and wore them proudly, sometimes even twisting them into festive little plaits.

But this was a scene from my life (perhaps life, including my own, did not exist either?) and it was hard to apply literary effects to it.

But, there we were, I was standing in front of a person, undoubtedly a woman, who had a very pronounced moustache. She wore it proudly, both when she appeared in the doorway, where whoever saw her from the stairs was blinded by the strong light from inside, and in the room, an improvised cosmetic salon, where in full light the eye took in the smallest detail.

She proudly offered me her brochure *Pearls of my Cosmetics*. Without waiting for the smile under her proud moustache to be coldly extinguished, as happens with disillusioned magicians, I immediately started fumbling in my handbag and my purse. But Kristina Verček suddenly closed her smile, like a weightless fan. For time passed inexorably in this salon where women came who wanted to live for a long time and not to grow old ... die?

'We'll talk about the book later. First a complete treatment!'

'Are you afraid of death?'

'No!'

He tapped his pencil on the half-written piece of paper and the *Atlas of World History* under it. Was he consoling or hurrying me?

But, I was not afraid. Nevertheless, I would have liked to tell him about that terrible feeling I have of being late ... the feeling that I have been overtaken and am losing my sense of being present. Neither here, nor there. With swinging legs. As on that far-off day, when I was waiting for my mother. Up a dark stairway, we had reached a door with a brass plate. Presumably with the word 'Dentist' engraved on it. A tall man in a white coat opened the door and with a broad sweep of his hand pointed my mother in a direction where she vanished after just two or three steps. He followed her and, unlike that heavy one, the second door closed soundlessly. I was left in the waiting-room, pressed between two doors. I sat down on a plastic chair and spent some time trying in vain to stop sliding on its smooth surface. I finally managed it by leaning the full weight of my body against it. I leafed through the magazine with pictures in it that my mother had bought on the way here. It was full of photographs of girls with thick hair, brushed away from their faces. I closed it and began to touch my own hair and then suddenly bent the top part of my body towards my knees. Under my knees I could make out the rest of my legs. They were swaying because they did not reach the yellow vinyl tiles. On my feet were my narrow shoes with blue satin bows. Suddenly the only thing in the world was their simple, persistent movement. The left-hand bow, then the right, left, then right ... a double pendulum.

Towards the chair, away from the chair, towards the chair, away from the chair.

Then there was a penetrating woman's scream.

I didn't want to run away. Nor did I feel pity. Not even that selfish feeling that separates the lucky from the unlucky, the healthy from the sick, the living from the dead. This is not happening to me, we think as we return from a funeral. We wipe our muddy shoes on the grass, draw our neck down between our shoulders, clench our hands into fists and push them deep into our pockets.

None of all that! I just felt the horror of a being that had not yet mastered a difficult and definitive task. If

107

I were to say: like a child staring at a complicated exercise when everyone else has written the answer in their books and left the classroom ... it would be insufficient and feeble. Inadequate for the horror of a little girl with swinging legs.

'So, children, who'll be the first to have the injection? Let me see.'

The smiling young woman with a white cap pinned onto her stiff hair-do which glistened with a gold sheen, looked over our heads.

'I will!'

I don't know whether I had already outgrown those tight little shoes by then, but I do remember that as I crossed the whole length of the room like a sleep-walker, I was rolling up the sleeve of one arm with my other hand.

I stood before the needle with my thin, bare muscle whose pale skin was slightly goose-fleshed. *'She's an excellent pupil, but somehow absent...'* I once heard my mother telling my father what my teacher had said about me. Let that be the reason why, as I volunteered to have the first injection, I said nothing about the fact that my mother, forewarned, had told the teacher (it was all written in a little note hidden in my pocket) that I should not have the vaccination since I was a year younger than the rest of the class and I had an allergy.

That was how I overcame my horror from the waiting-room with the yellow vinyl squares. The next day, I had an arm the muscle of which was like a long balloon pumped full of inner fire. How much it hurt, how long it lasted and how many reproaches I heard in my half-fever ... is no longer important, nor do I remember. I only know that after staying away for a long time, I stepped proudly into the classroom. Present! Not even seeking confirmation of my feelings in the face of my teacher, the colour of whose eyes I do not recall, but I remember the thick black fringe above them.

'And so, ladies, who will be first?'

Mrs Kristina Verček was standing between two couches. I was on the left-hand one, on the other was a young woman who had arrived two or three minutes after me, bringing the scent of an unfamiliar perfume into the room.

The owner of the proud moustache stood between the two of us. In her right hand she was holding a moist cosmetic mask, waiting for us to decide whose face to place it on first.

'I will!'

The woman on the other couch could not know that this appropriation of the first place was more the result of a distant event than haste. But, when I looked round at her, she returned my glance with an expression of perfect understanding.

We looked at each other the way fair and dark women look at each other, blond and dark-haired, the way women never look at one another if they represent a sub-variant or sub-group. We looked at each other like women in a maternity ward, each with her own child inside her.

I stepped out of Kristina Verček's salon into a cool, violet evening, but my skin was glowing from the *complete treatment*. Behind me in the room was the mask and under it the face of the dark-haired woman. Her body was stretched out like a figure lying in a sarcophagus.

Once again I became an irregular reader of *Pearls of My Cosmetics*. I never read the brochure that crowned the complete treatment and tripled the cost of a visit to the salon. I gave it to my colleague who returned from her long weekend like a butterfly, but without the promised gift. When the city was surrounded, she was driven out of her apartment on the other side of the iron ring. She arrived with nothing in her hands or pockets. She had only one, right, shoe. She had aged overnight. She was no longer a butterfly.

I came across the face of the dark-haired woman once more.

'Isn't she still lying there, under the mask,' I wondered, catching sight of her at the airport, just as my flight was announced.

She was sitting with three men who were discussing something animatedly, looking in her direction the whole time. They were even leaning towards her across the table, but she did not respond with a typical woman's gesture of moving away. Between her index and middle fingers she had an unlit cigarette. She was touching her upper lip with the tip of her thumb. Her chin was tucked into her neck, as though she was trying to see how far she could bend her head without moving her body. And she was smiling. As women do when they let men talk, talk, talk. Then they just sigh and say *Please*. She lowered her hand with the unlit cigarette and the tip of her thumb slipped gently from her moist upper lip.

I am going down a long, glass tunnel. I clasp my bag to me. I turn round. A dark and a fair woman are looking at one another again. One is in a hurry. The other is sitting, smiling. Is there a *Please* and a sigh after this?

I saw a photograph of this face, taken for a passport or identity card, in an obituary, a year after the city was surrounded.

We look at one another. Now: one lady absent and one present!

The obituary informed me that the young woman had passed away in Rome, after a brief, serious illness. There were three names listed as *bereaved*. As when someone dies in one of those rare, urban families that thin out over the years, waiting to gather again at last on the other side and for no one to be listed as *bereaved*.

Three months later, the same face in another obituary. This time the photograph was like those taken out of a family album. There was someone's hand on one shoulder. Her appearance was softer and gentler than in the first obituary. As though she was turning towards the hand that touched her shoulder.

She smiled the way she had done that evening when our eyes met and there was a hand with a prepared mask between us.

This time the obituary announced that her cremated remains, brought from Rome, had been placed in a grave in the city cemetery. Two names were listed as *bereaved*. Just two more and then they would all be together.

He sometimes travels out of the besieged city. That requires a special pass. People travel by transporter-planes that fly to Ancona from where food and medical aid are flown to the besieged city from all over the world. In addition to food and medical aid, photographers and journalists come, and questionnaires like the one that asked *How would you like to die?*

At the airport in Ancona he has to wait for hours for a place in the plane. But, there is plenty for him to see while he waits. He sees people coming and going, their purpose and lack of purpose.

On the day when he had to wait ten hours for a flight into the besieged city, he saw a man who spent the whole time he was waiting sitting between two bags, with a strange-shaped box clasped in his lap.

When, finally, the loudspeaker announced the flight and called out the names of ten of the hundred or so passengers who had registered, those two bags were among the first to reach the soldier checking passes and weighing luggage. In addition to his body weight, a passenger could take only a further thirty kilograms into the besieged city. The two bags did not weigh more than thirty kilograms, but the clearly bad-tempered soldier who weighed them wanted the strange-shaped box to be placed on the scales as well. A quiet, but acrimonious argument ensued, the soldier was increasingly insistent and increasingly bad-tempered and there was a hold-up, which meant that bad temper also began to spread through the other nine passengers in the queue. One stared fixedly at the box, and then whispered something anxiously to the passenger immediately next to him. Soon a soft whisper passed down the queue and came to an end in a strange silence. Only the soldier persisted in his original mood and soon the box found itself on the scales, squeezed between the two bags. With it the luggage weighed somewhat more than the permitted thirty kilograms. Before the triumphant expression on the soldier's face had turned into a loud statement, the hand which had rested on the strange box for the whole ten hours of waiting had already opened the first bag and hurriedly taken from it a large can of pineapple and a long box holding ten packets of cigarettes. At last the weight was less than the allowance. Perhaps he hadn't needed to remove the cigarettes? But the passenger was no longer looking at either the scales or the soldier. He grabbed his two bags, thrusting the strange shaped box into one of them.

The strange box was travelling along the glass tunnel, which led to the aeroplane. The ashes of the young woman who had once lain on my right, in Kristina Verček's cosmetic salon, were travelling to the besieged city. At the cost of a large can of pineapple! Or at the cost of ten packs of cigarettes.

'It would be good to fall asleep like this,' a woman's voice had said that day, in the cosmetic salon. Mine or that woman's? The dark or the fair woman? It was certainly not Kristina Verček's voice. Hers had already passed from soprano through the phase of mature female alto and become baritone. But, nor could it have been mine. Because there was already a moist mask on my face and under it my lips were tightly closed.

But, once you step into a room without windows, full of mysterious tinctures kept in attractively shaped glass jars, once you listen to an empty room and the constant hum behind the distant partitions, once you feel a slight shudder running from the nape of your neck down your spine while the layer of correcting fluid dries on the word that has already been written ... then anything is possible. It could be that the voice had after all come through my tightly closed lips and that it had not said *fall asleep* but *die*.

'So?'

'Must I?'

'What ... die?'

'No ... must I answer that question?'

'No. But you've already answered three questions as though you hadn't.'

'I don't know, I can't say, I don't understand the question ... here, have a look yourself.'

'I know, I know ... let it be as I said: at Kristina Verček's.'

'This is meant for people abroad. They'll read it. I'm afraid that even here no one, or hardly anyone, knows who that lady is ... what was it ... Verček? But, let's see what can be done with that ... what it looks like ... What it means ..'

'I don't know exactly. You're both inside and outside. Covered up and uncovered. And you don't see anyone but others see you but that doesn't bother you ... somehow ...'

'Shall I put "in my sleep"?'

'Maybe. What did you put yourself?'

'In my sleep.'

Was he repeating my question like an echo or was he confirming that that was what he had replied?

'Fine, let it be "in my sleep".'

'Don't say "let it be". Later you'll change your mind but the answer will already be at the printer's, and a long way off, you won't be able to grumble and plead ... and it'll all be my fault.'

'No, that's just what I wanted to say ... in my sleep ... But couldn't they have asked "when" you want and not "how" you want to die?'

'They could have, if they had consulted you. But they didn't! Come on, that's enough, it's late.'

He wrote the answer beside the printed question. Folded the paper and wrapped it round my photograph, which had been lying on the little table between us. At last the photograph and the answers were in the pink envelope. He ran his hand over it when it was sealed, smoothing it, as though testing its thickness. He put it down beside the pen and burning candle.

'Shall we blow it out? It's nearly midnight.'

'You go. I'll be along in a minute. I'll just ...'

He is already in the bedroom. He has taken the

116

Times Atlas of World History with him. Perhaps, by hurrying me up, he has elicited an unwanted reply? The envelope is already sealed.

I bend my head towards my knees and look down my legs at my feet, resting on the floor this time, where there are no blue satin bows. Just warm fur slippers, which he brought me back from Ancona after that first terrible winter in the besieged city. The next day, as soon as he had left the house, I would look in the wardrobe for my unworn shoes, bought four years earlier.

***

At roughly the time when we received two copies of the magazine with the photographs and the answers of a hundred inhabitants of the besieged city (my colleage-butterfly who had aged overnight called the magazine ... *delectable ... aaah ... the coup of the season in the besieged city)*, I met Kristina Verček. She did not recognise me. But I recognised her.

We passed each other and I suddenly turned round. Unfortunately, it is impossible to judge from someone's back whether the face on its other side has ordinary whiskers, let alone a proud moustache. But, as the former owner of the proud moustache was coming towards me, for a fraction of a second, it had seemed to me that she had none. The bags

117

under my eyes from that evening had remained. If that really had been Kristina Verček, it seemed that many months of living in the besieged city had bequeathed her rapid old age while depriving her of her proud moustache. Whether her voice was still modulated in three tones, I could not tell, as I watched her departing back.

That day I had not put on the shoes I had bought because the shop assistant made me feel uncomfortable. But I had already begun to wear them.

In the besieged city one walks over rubble and splinters. Shoes wear out quickly. Even those bought involuntarily are welcome.

I did not meet the shop assistant with the stern twins behind her large spectacles. Or else I did not recognise her. But once, in the queue for water (one waits for water in long queues here), I heard a brief conversation between two women:

'Are you working?'

'No. Our shop has closed. I'm waiting.'

Very few shops are open in the besieged city. On the whole, only those with bread or some left-over nonsense from the time when the city was not besieged. It would have been sad, however, if the person waiting was the one who had once said so impatiently:

'Well, madam, have we decided? I have other customers waiting!'

I sometimes leaf through the magazine in which I deposited my answers. Whenever I catch sight of my photograph it seems to me that I am about to step out of it. This impression may be verified in the Museum of Modern Art in New York. A colleague of mine, the office entertainer, somehow got himself to Atlanta. He calls from time to time, when telephone connections with the besieged city are working. He has seen the magazine, although he still does not visit museums. Several dozen copies have made their way to all the important international news agencies. I asked him how I looked in the photograph.

'Like someone with a "troublet", like at 8.30 am ... and your jacket has one as well ...'

He did not know that when I asked him how I looked in that photograph, what I had wanted to know was whether I was in it at all. And so he did not know why I had not flinched at his observation about the jacket in the pocket of which, when we worked in the same editorial board, he would often leave a scrap of paper with the message:

'Three times too big? Am I right?'

I did not ask him about the answers. I did not have to confirm them in the Museum of Modern Art in New York. Both there and here, beside the question *How would you like to die?* lay my final answer *In my sleep*.

119

The same hand that had written my answer had written as his own reply to the same question: *I don't know.*

One of the hundred inhabitants of the besieged city who had been asked had already died. She had died of a serious illness. In the besieged city serious illnesses develop rapidly. As though our life is a gramophone record turning at the wrong speed; too fast. Like a tape that someone impatient is playing *speeded up.*

I checked in the magazine. There it said that she had wanted to die without a lengthy illness and with nice memories. Perhaps her serious illness had not lasted long. Although it is difficult in the case of a serious illness and a besieged city, to determine what is short and what long. One could hope that she had at least died with nice memories. Her face is still in the photograph, beside her answers. She does not look like a person intending to step out of it. An agreeable older lady, smiling proudly, her body wrapped in a smart fur coat.

My friend the writer, who says that characters do not exist and explains to copy editors that one 'easy' is not the same as another 'easy', had answered the question *How would you like to die?* with the slightly longer word for 'easily' in our language. But, for an American, one 'easy' is the same as another. Hence a visitor to the Museum of Modern Art may read that my friend the writer wanted to die *easily.* He understands that, but the writer does not. That word introduces confusion into the writer's answer. Can wishes of

120

this kind be expressed in a foreign language, particularly one that does not distinguish one 'easily' from another?

Maybe one should not answer such questionnaires any more, even with the promise of the appealing possibility that our face, photographed, will be displayed to the gaze of the whole wide world. They do not encourage you to confess whom you love, they do not have the charming effect of children's confessionals, and afterwards those answers lie like involuntarily purchased shoes in a wardrobe.

The city is still besieged. The nights are often long and empty. Then I suffer from insomnia and the bags under my eyes are deep. He tells me that he thinks I elude sleep and not that sleep eludes me. On particularly empty, silent nights, I see a mask from under which the nice face of the dark woman reappears. She smiles. She says nothing. But I have already learned to read the invitation between the lines. I want to ask whose voice it was that evening that said it would be good to fall asleep.

The mask changes into a layer of correcting fluid. The wiped out word peers out from underneath it. I am overwhelmed by the same horror as the little girl whose legs swung over the yellow vinyl squares, outside the door from behind which a terrible scream is heard. The scream is wiped out by silence and the horror in me becomes still greater.

One morning, after such a night, I asked him:

'How much would the ash weigh if my body was cremated?'

'Have you got a less weighty question?'

He pinched the lobe of my ear, kissed me on my lips and left me without an answer but with warmth, in my ear lobe, and the sharp taste of toothpaste on my lips.

Besides, the hand I write with has healed. If any new questions should ever arrive, I shall write my answers myself. I'm writing all of this with my own hand. I have placed the *Times Atlas of World History* under the sheets of paper. It is night. Tonight, in the Museum of Modern Art in New York, the answer extorted from me keeps vigil.

Best of the Balkans – Istros Books' titles for 2014

Hamam Balkania by Vladislav Bajac (Serbia) translated by Randall A. Major – An exploration into the power structures of the Ottoman Empire, juxtaposed with musings on contemporary concepts of identity and faith. A truly ambitious book that rewards the reader with insights into some of the great questions of our time. ISBN: 978-1908236142

Mission London by Alek Popov (Bulgaria) translated by Daniela and Charles Edward Gill de Mayol de Lupe - Combining the themes of corruption, confusion and outright incompetence, Popov masterly brings together multiple plot lines in a sumptuous carnival of frenzy and futile vanity, allowing the illusions and delusions of post-communist society to be reflected in their glorious absurdity! ISBN: 978-1908236180

False Apocalypse by Fatos Lubonja (Albania) translated by John Hodgson – 1997, a tragic year in the history of post-communist Albania. This is one man's story of how the world's most isolated country emerged from Stalinist dictatorship and fell victim to a plague of corruption and flawed 'pyramid' financial schemes which brought people to the edge of ruin. ISBN: 978-908236197

The Great War by Aleksandar Gatalica (Serbia) translated by Will Firth – In the centenary year of the start of WWI, we finally have a Serbian author taking on the themes of a war that was started by a Serb assassin's bullet. Following the destinies of over seventy characters, on all warring sides, Gatalica depicts the destinies of winners and losers, generals and opera singers, soldiers and spies, in the conflict that marked the beginning of the Twentieth Century. ISBN: 978-1908236203